YEARLING BOOKS

Since 1966, Yearling has been the

leading name in classic and award-winning

literature for young readers.

With a wide variety of titles,

Yearling paperbacks entertain, inspire,

and encourage a love of reading.

VISIT

WWW.RANDOMHOUSE.COM/KIDS

**TO FIND THE PERFECT BOOK, PLAY GAMES,
AND MEET FAVORITE AUTHORS!**

OTHER YEARLING BOOKS YOU WILL ENJOY

BLACK-EYED SUSAN, *Jennifer Armstrong*

CHARLOTTE'S ROSE, *A. E. Cannon*

THE TRUE PRINCE, *J. B. Cheaney*

JUMP SHIP TO FREEDOM
James Lincoln Collier and Christopher Collier

RODZINA, *Karen Cushman*

JACOB'S RESCUE: A HOLOCAUST STORY
Malka Drucker and Michael Halperin

JOHNNY TREMAIN, *Esther Forbes*

THE IRON DRAGON NEVER SLEEPS, *Stephen Krensky*

MR. TUCKET, *Gary Paulsen*

THANK YOU, DR. MARTIN LUTHER KING, JR.!, *Eleanora Tate*

Penny from Heaven

JENNIFER L. HOLM

A YEARLING BOOK

Published by Yearling, an imprint of Random House Children's Books
a division of Random House, Inc., New York

If you purchased this book without a cover you should be aware that this book is stolen
property. It was reported as "unsold and destroyed" to the publisher and neither the author
nor the publisher has received any payment for this "stripped book."

"Pennies from Heaven" by Johnny Burke and Arthur Johnston © 1936 (renewed)
CHAPPELL & CO., INC. All rights reserved. Used by permission.
Warner Bros. Publications U.S., Inc., Miami, Florida 33014.

Photos courtesy of: National Archives and Records Administration, College Park,
Maryland (p. 262). Ely Greenfield, used by permission of *Una Storia Segreta,* a project of the
American Italian Historical Association, Western Regional Chapter (p. 261). Lake County
Museum/CORBIS (p. 265). All other photos from the personal collection
of Beverly Ann Scaccia Holm, used by permission.

Copyright © 2006 by Jennifer L. Holm

All rights reserved. No part of this book may be reproduced or transmitted in any form
or by any means, electronic or mechanical, including photocopying, recording, or by any
information storage and retrieval system, without the written permission of the
publisher, except where permitted by law. For information address
Random House Books for Young Readers.

Yearling and the jumping horse design are registered trademarks of Random House, Inc.

Visit us on the Web! www.randomhouse.com/kids

Educators and librarians, for a variety of teaching tools, visit us at
www.randomhouse.com/teachers

ISBN: 978-0-375-83689-3

Reprinted by arrangement with Random House Books for Young Readers

Printed in the United States of America

December 2007

20 19 18 17 16 15 14 13 12

First Yearling Edition

For our Henry,
the best fella ever

Contents

A long time ago
A million years BC
The best things in life
Were absolutely free.
But no one appreciated
A sky that was always blue.
And no one congratulated
A moon that was always new.
So it was planned that they would vanish now and then
And you must pay before you get them back again.
That's what storms were made for
And you shouldn't be afraid for
Every time it rains it rains
Pennies from heaven.
Don't you know each cloud contains
Pennies from heaven.
You'll find your fortune falling
All over town.
Be sure that your umbrella is upside down.
Trade them for a package of sunshine and flowers.
If you want the things you love
You must have showers.
So when you hear it thunder
Don't run under a tree.
There'll be pennies from heaven for you and me.

—"Pennies from Heaven" by Johnny Burke and Arthur Johnston

Penny from Heaven

CHAPTER ONE

Best Seat in the House

Me-me says that Heaven is full of fluffy white clouds and angels.

That sounds pretty swell, but how can you sit on a cloud? Wouldn't you fall right through and smack onto the ground? Like Frankie always says, angels have wings, so what do they have to worry about?

My idea of Heaven has nothing to do with clouds or angels. In my Heaven there's butter pecan ice cream and swimming pools and baseball games. The Brooklyn Dodgers always win, and I have the best seat in the house, right behind the Dodgers' dugout. That's the only advantage that I can see to being dead: You get the best seat in the house.

I think about Heaven a lot. Not because of the

usual reasons, though. I'm only eleven, and I don't plan on dying until I'm at least a hundred. It's just that I'm named after that Bing Crosby song "Pennies from Heaven," and when you're named after something, you can't help but think about it.

See, my father was crazy about Bing Crosby, and that's why everyone calls me Penny instead of Barbara Ann Falucci, which is what's on my birth certificate. No one ever calls me Barbara, except teachers, and sometimes even I forget that it's my real name.

I guess it could be worse. I could be called Clementine, which was the name of another Bing Crosby song that my father really liked.

I don't think I'd make a very good Clementine. Then again, who would?

CHAPTER TWO

The Lucky Bean

Uncle Dominic is sitting in his car.

It's a 1940 Plymouth Roadking. It's black with chrome trim, and the hubcaps are so shiny, you could use them as a mirror. Uncle Dominic pays my cousin Frankie to shine them up. It's an awfully nice car; everybody says so. But then, it's kind of hard to miss. It's been parked in the side yard of my grandmother Falucci's house for as long as I can remember.

Uncle Dominic lives right there in his car. Nobody in the family thinks it's weird that Uncle Dominic lives in his car, or if they do, nobody ever says anything. It's 1953, and it's not exactly normal for people in New Jersey to live in cars. Most people around here live in houses. But Uncle Dominic's kind of a hermit. He also likes to wear slippers instead of shoes. Once I asked him why.

"They're comfortable," he said.

Besides living in the car and wearing slippers, Uncle Dominic's my favorite uncle, and I have a lot of uncles. Sometimes I lose track of them.

"Hey, Princess," Uncle Dominic calls.

I lean through the window and hear the announcer on the portable radio. Uncle Dominic likes to listen to ball games in the car. There's a pillow and a ratty-looking blanket on the backseat. Uncle Dominic says the car's the only place he can get any rest. He has a lot of trouble falling asleep.

"Hi, Uncle Dominic," I say.

"Game's on," he says.

I start to open the back door, but Uncle Dominic says, "You can sit up front."

Uncle Dominic's very particular about who's allowed to sit in his car. Most people have to sit in the back, although Uncle Nunzio always sits up front. I don't think anyone ever tells Uncle Nunzio what to do.

"Who's winning?" I ask.

"Bums are ahead."

I love the Brooklyn Dodgers, and so does Uncle Dominic. We call them Dem Bums. Most people around here like the New York Yankees or the Giants, but not us.

Uncle Dominic is staring out the window, like he's really in the ballpark and watching the game from the bleachers. He's handsome, with dark hair and brown eyes. Everyone says he looks just like my father. I don't remember my father because he died when I was just a baby, but I've seen photographs, and Uncle Dominic does look like him, except sadder.

"Got something for you," Uncle Dominic says.

All my uncles give me presents. Uncle Nunzio gives me fur muffs, and Uncle Ralphie gives me candy, and Uncle Paulie brings me fancy perfumes, and Uncle Sally gives me horseshoes. It's like Christmas all the time.

Uncle Dominic hands me something that looks like a big dark-brown bean.

"What is it?"

"It's a lucky bean," he says. Uncle Dominic is superstitious. "Just found it this morning. It was packed away with some old things. I got it for your father before he died, but I never had a chance to give it to him. I want you to have it."

"Where'd you get it?" I ask.

"Florida," he says.

Uncle Dominic loves Florida and goes to Vero Beach every winter, probably because it's too cold to live in the car then. Even though he lives in this car, he has another car that he uses for driving, a 1950 Cadillac Coupe de Ville. Frankie says he bets Uncle Dominic has a girl down in Florida, but I kind of don't think so. Most women want a new Frigidaire, not a backseat.

"Put it in your pocket," he says. "It'll keep you safe."

The lucky bean is big and lumpy. It feels heavy, not the kind of thing to put in a pocket, but Uncle Dominic has this look about his eyes like he might just die if I don't, and because he is my favorite uncle, I do what I always do.

I smile and say, "Thanks, Uncle Dominic."

For a moment the strain leaves his eyes.

"Anything for you, Princess," he says. "Anything."

It's a hot, sticky June day. School is out, and for the first time in months I don't have to worry about Veronica Goodman being mean to me. I used to like school, until this year. I probably wouldn't have survived if Mrs. Ellenburg, the librarian, hadn't let me hide out in the library. Lucky for me, Veronica Goodman doesn't like to read.

The lucky bean rubs in my pocket as I walk down the street toward my house. I live with my mother and my other grandparents, Me-me and

Pop-pop, and my poodle, Scarlett O'Hara. Even though she's named after a famous lady in a boring movie, Scarlett O'Hara isn't very ladylike. Scarlett has bad breath and likes to chase squirrels and has taken to tinkling on the good carpet in the parlor lately, not to mention other things she shouldn't be doing.

Pop-pop's sitting in the parlor when I get home. He's listening to the radio and has got it turned up loud enough that the whole neighborhood can hear it. His favorite program is *Fibber McGee and Molly,* although he'll sleep through just about any program these days. We don't have a television set because Me-me says they're too expensive, which means they'll probably buy one right after I graduate high school and move out.

"I'm back," I announce.

"What's that?" he asks.

"I said, 'I'm back,' Pop-pop," I say loudly.

"What?" he asks. "What?"

Pop-pop's a little deaf. Me-me says he's been deaf ever since 1918, when he came home from Europe with shrapnel in his leg. She says he left the best part of him somewhere in France, along with his ability to listen to anyone.

There's a bad smell in the room.

"Pop-pop, what's that smell?" I ask.

"Sure, I'll take an iced tea," he says.

I spot the little brown lump behind the love seat. It looks kind of like the lucky bean Uncle Dominic gave me. Scarlett O'Hara's nowhere in sight.

"Look what Scarlett did," I say.

"Darn animal," he grumbles. Pop-pop can hear okay when he wants to. "That dog of yours is sneakier than the Japs."

Even though we're in a war right now in Korea, Pop-pop still loves talking about World War II, especially Pearl Harbor and how the Japanese attacked us when we were sleeping. He says it's the worst thing that's ever happened on American soil. No one saw it coming.

"Downright cowardly is what it was," he always says.

I don't remember the war because I was too small, but I sure am glad we won. Eating breakfast in our house is tough enough without having to worry about being bombed by the Japanese.

"Penny!" Me-me calls from the kitchen.

We have a two-story house. Me-me and Pop-pop live in the top part and Mother and I live in the bottom. My grandparents have their own bedroom, bathroom, and parlor, but they take all their meals downstairs with us because there's just the one kitchen. In fact, Me-me does most of the cooking, since my mother has to work. She's a secretary at a truck factory.

Me-me is standing with her back to me, facing the stove, when I walk into the kitchen. Her hair is going gray, and she's got it up in a bun. She's wearing a cotton dress with a red cherry print. Me-me loves colorful prints, and she also has a dress with cabbage roses, one with fruit segments, and another one with daisies. My favorite is the dress with the Hawaiian palm trees. I think it would be fun to go someplace like Hawaii. It's got to be more exciting than New Jersey.

I don't have to look in the pot she's stirring to know it's peas and onions. The smell fills the air. Me-me likes to boil vegetables until they are pure mush and every bit of flavor is gone. I didn't even know peas could be sweet until I tasted them fresh off the vine at my grandmother Falucci's house.

"What's for dinner?" I ask.

"Liver," she says, and I have to make myself not groan.

Me-me's liver is worse than her pot roast, which is worse than her beef Stroganoff, and you don't even want to know about her meat loaf.

"Set the table, please," Me-me says.

I take the green glass dishes out of the cabinet and carry them to the dining room, where there's just a table and chairs and a sideboard. On the sideboard is an old clock and a framed photograph of my mother and father on their wedding day. We don't talk about my father in this house because it upsets my mother. I guess she's never gotten over him dying like he did and leaving her with a baby. She used to be a nurse at the hospital where he was taken when he got sick, but she said after he died, she couldn't go back there, that there were too many sad memories.

In the wedding photograph, my father is wearing a dark suit, and his arm is around my mother's waist as if he's scared she's going to run away. My mother's wearing a white satin dress and carrying a bouquet of sweet peas. Her hair is long, past her shoulders, and curled like a movie star's. She's smiling at the camera like she's the luckiest girl in the world.

She looks so happy, I almost don't recognize her.

Me-me has been staring at the clock for the last half hour while Pop-pop and I watch the liver and peas and onions get cold. Scarlett O'Hara is sitting next to Pop-pop's chair, waiting for something to fall from his plate, which is usually a good bet.

Pop-pop takes a long slurp of iced tea and burps loudly. A moment later he burps again.

"Pop-pop!" I say.

"What?" he says with a scowl.

Honestly, I don't know which is more embarrassing—Scarlett O'Hara doing her business in the house or Pop-pop burping all the time. And Mother wonders why I never want to have friends over for a slumber party.

The front door opens, and Me-me straightens her shoulders and sits a little taller.

"Sorry I'm late, Mother," my mother says, unpinning her hat and slipping into her place at the table.

She's wearing a plain navy-blue suit and has wavy golden-brown hair, cut short, just below her ears. She uses Tangee rouge on her cheeks and a little bit of red lipstick. The Tangee rouge is the fanciest thing about her.

"Do you know what time it is, Eleanor?" Me-me asks, looking pointedly at the clock. "It's seven-thirty, that's what time it is. What kind of place is that man running?"

"Mr. Hendrickson had some last-minute dictation," my mother says.

Me-me looks at my plate and says, "Eat your peas, Penny."

I take a bite, forcing myself to swallow. They're just awful. They taste like something you would feed someone you were trying to torture.

Pop-pop is poking the liver with his fork. "I thought you said we were having steak," he complains. "This looks like liver."

"Hi, Bunny," my mother says to me, and I can hear the tiredness in her voice. "How was your day?"

Bunny is her nickname for me. She said she took one look at me in the hospital and I looked so small and sweet that she knew I was a bunny.

"Look what I got," I say. I dig in my pocket and pull out the lucky bean and put it on the flower-print tablecloth.

Pop-pop starts choking when he sees it. "Did you bring a dog turd to the table?"

Scarlett O'Hara barks as if to deny she has anything to do with it.

"It's a lucky bean," I explain. "Uncle Dominic gave it to me."

"Lucky bean?" Me-me scoffs. "The only lucky thing—"

"Mother," my mother says in a warning voice.

"Your father's people," Me-me says to me with

a shake of her head. What she means is that they're Italian, and Catholic.

Me-me and Pop-pop are plain old American, and Methodist. They go to church every Sunday, and usually make me go too. My mother doesn't go to any church at all.

"Here's a good one, Penny," Pop-pop says. He loves jokes. "Why does the new Italian navy have glass-bottom boats?"

"Why?"

"To see the *old* Italian navy!" he hoots. "Get it? Their boats are at the bottom of the ocean!"

My mother looks down at her plate and sighs.

"Mother," I say, "Uncle Ralphie says he'll hire me and Frankie to work at the store a few days a week. Can I? It could be my summer job."

Uncle Ralphie is one of my father's brothers. He owns a butcher shop.

"What will you be doing?" she asks.

"Sweeping up, stacking, delivering groceries."

"Deliver groceries to strange people's houses? You're a young girl," Me-me says, sounding appalled.

"I don't think so, Penny," Mother says, which is what she always says.

My mother's afraid of just about everything that involves fun. I can't go swimming because there might be polio in the public pool. I can't go to the movie theater because I might catch polio there, too. I can't go on the bumper cars because I could hurt my neck. Don't do this, Penny! Don't do that, Penny! It's too dangerous, Penny! Anything could happen, Penny! Sometimes I want to say that the most dangerous thing in my life is Me-me's cooking.

"Please? We'll be working at the store most of the time," I say.

My mother and Me-me share a long look. Mother doesn't like it when I spend a lot of time with my father's family, although she tries not to show it. The two sides of the family don't get along. I've never even seen them in the same room together. I know it wasn't always this way because of the famous story my Italian relatives like to tell about my parents' engagement party. Apparently Uncle Dominic used to be a real practical joker, especially with Mother. At the party he gave my mother a box with a big pink bow. My mother opened the box expecting to find candy, but lying there in tissue paper was a pair of lamb's eyes.

"So you can keep an eye on Freddy," Uncle Dominic told her.

It's hard to believe that she laughed as much as they all say she did.

"Please?" I plead. "I'll be real careful."

Me-me shrugs, and my mother turns to me and says, "All right. But tell your uncle that I said Frankie has to go with you on the deliveries. Understand?"

"You bet!" I say, and I can't keep the excitement out of my voice.

Me-me says, "Bah. That boy?"

Everything is quiet for a moment, and I push a few mushy gray peas around on my plate. Next to me Pop-pop burps, and we all look at him at the same time.

"What?" he says.

"The bills are due," Me-me tells my mother.

My mother gets up and goes to the front hall. When she returns, there is an envelope in her hand. She hands it to Me-me.

Me-me studies it and says, "Slave wages." Then she goes into the kitchen and takes down a white jar with a picture of a cow and the words "Milk Money" on it and drops the check in. It's where Me-me keeps money for grocery shopping.

"A perfectly good education being wasted," Me-me says.

"Don't start, Mother," my mother says. "I've had a long day."

But Me-me is like Scarlett O'Hara when she

gets it into her head to chew something to pieces.

"You were the best nurse in your graduating class," Me-me says.

"Enough," my mother snaps.

"I've held my tongue too long as it is," Me-me snaps back.

My mother stands up without another word and walks out of the room, slamming the door. Me-me gets up and carries her plate into the kitchen and bangs it on the counter. Scarlett O'Hara starts barking and Pop-pop says loudly, "Where's the steak? I thought you said we were having steak."

And me?

I just sit there, listening to the silence.

CHAPTER THREE

Mrs. Morelli's Brains

The sign outside says FALUCCI'S MARKET. BEST
PORK AND MEAT CUTS.

When I open the door, a little bell rings.

"Look who it is," Uncle Ralphie calls from
behind the long marble counter.

He's wearing an apron and talking to a slender
woman with stockings that have a tear near the
ankle. A little boy with a grubby neck is clinging
to one of her legs, and another kid with a smear
of jam on his face is wrapped around her other
leg. She turns, and I see the round bump of her
stomach.

"Mrs. Chickalos," Uncle Ralphie says grandly,
"do you know my beautiful niece, Penny? My late
brother Freddy's girl, God rest his soul."

Mrs. Chickalos turns to me and says in a soft voice, "How do you do?"

"Glad to know you," I say.

Uncle Ralphie turns back to Mrs. Chickalos. "Now, you're sure you don't need any ham? I got a real nice ham in the back, just delicious."

"I can't afford that," she says in the same soft voice.

"Don't you worry about that, you hear me?" he says. "You just take care of these beautiful children of yours."

Actually, the kids could stand a bath before anyone would call them beautiful, but that's Uncle Ralphie for you.

I watch as my uncle cuts and wraps a large chunk of ham and puts it in the bag. Then he wraps up a whole chicken and sticks it in there, saying, "The bones'll make a good stock. You can get two, maybe three, meals out of it." He winks. "Good for the baby."

She reaches into her handbag, but he just waves her away. "I'm not going anywhere."

"Thank you, Mr. Falucci," she says.

He beams at her. "My pleasure."

She gathers up her bag and walks out of the store, the kids hanging on to her skirt.

"Ralphie," Aunt Fulvia says as soon as the door closes.

"What?" Uncle Ralphie says. "They're good people, *patanella mia*."

Patanella mia is Uncle Ralphie's nickname for Aunt Fulvia. He says it means "my little potato." A lot of my Italian relatives have nicknames.

"'Good' doesn't put dinner on the table," she snaps back.

Uncle Ralphie's always giving people food on credit, and it drives Aunt Fulvia crazy. She's the one who really runs the store. Aunt Fulvia sits on a little stool behind the register at the door like a sentry, ringing up purchases, putting half the money in the till and half in the pocket of her skirt. Frankie says that way the government doesn't get the money.

"I suppose she still hasn't paid us what she owes from last month," Aunt Fulvia says, and then leans over to look at the sleeping baby in the carriage next to her. Baby Gloria can sleep through anything, even Aunt Fulvia.

Uncle Ralphie throws up his hands.

"We'll be in the poorhouse at this rate," Aunt Fulvia mutters.

Uncle Ralphie may be a softy, but he always

gets paid back eventually. Every now and then things will just show up at the store on the back step, like a box of records or some macaroons, and Uncle Ralphie will give a low whistle and say, "Look what some little bird has left."

The bell on the door rings and Jack Teitelzweig is standing there. Jack's two years ahead of me at school, and I don't know him very well, but his brother Stanley is in my grade.

"If it isn't Jack Teitelzweig!" Uncle Ralphie says. "I got your mother's order all ready."

"Hi, Penny," Jack says, glancing back at me.

Before I can say anything, the bell on the door rings again and my cousin Frankie bursts in, out of breath.

"I'm here!" he announces.

"You're late," Aunt Fulvia tells him.

Frankie's twelve, with dark hair and brown eyes like me. Most people think we're brother and sister, which I don't mind except when he gets into trouble. His mother, Aunt Teresa, is my father's sister.

"I had to help Ma with the baby," he says. Frankie's got a baby brother, Michael, who's two months old.

"You're changing diapers now?" Aunt Fulvia asks.

"Sure I am!" he says, his eyes wide and innocent as an altar boy's. He's had a lot of practice.
He's been an altar boy at St. Anthony's for a few
years now. He likes it okay, except he sometimes
falls asleep during the services.

"You're full of excuses, huh, kid?" Aunt Fulvia
says, and then shakes her head. "You two go pack
up those deliveries."

I hear Jack say to Uncle Ralphie, "Thanks, Mr.
Falucci," and then he's gone.

"Say, I think she believed you," I tell Frankie.

"'Course she did," he says with a sly wink.

Frankie's father, Uncle Angelo, spent some
time in jail a few years ago. He robbed a five-and-
dime store, but he wasn't a very good criminal.
When he robbed the store, he also took a bunch of
candy bars. He ate the candy and threw the wrappers out of his car window as he made his getaway,
so the police just followed the trail of candy bar
wrappers and caught him. Frankie's crazy about his
father and thinks being a criminal would be neat. I
worry about him sometimes.

We go back to the meat locker. The store is
mostly a butcher shop, but we also sell groceries
and fresh produce. Over at the butcher table,
Uncle Dominic is wearing a bloody apron and
grinding beef into hamburger with the hand

grinder. He likes working in the back. This way he doesn't have to deal with customers, which is just as well. I don't think his slippers would be good for business.

"Hi, Princess," Uncle Dominic says to me.

"What's the big buzz?" I ask.

"The mound's looking real good for Dem Bums," he says. "I think we've got a shot at the Series."

"Yeah," Frankie scoffs. "A shot at losing."

The Dodgers have made it into the World Series before, but they always lose. The Yankees beat them last year after seven games. It's enough to make a Bums fan cry.

"They'll pull through, you'll see. You gotta have faith," Uncle Dominic says, and I want to believe him.

See, a long time ago, before I was born, Uncle Dominic played baseball. He was in the minor leagues and played all over—Newport News, Virginia, and Greenville, North Carolina. He was invited to spring training with the Dodgers, but then something happened, and he quit baseball, and now he works for Uncle Ralphie in the store. He's still pals with a few of the fellas, and sometimes he has good gossip. I don't know why anyone would trade catching balls for chopping up meat, but then it's just one more thing I'll probably never understand.

Uncle Ralphie walks into the room.

"You two kiddies think you can carry all this?" he asks us.

"Penny's got to carry that hair around all day," Frankie snickers, and I smack him.

Me-me thinks I pay too much attention to baseball and not enough to fashion. She got it into her head to give me a Toni home perm at the beginning of the summer and left the solution on too long, and now my hair looks like brown cotton wool.

"All right, then," Uncle Ralphie says, and he lowers his glasses to the end of his nose and goes over the list with us. "The bag with the pork loin is for Mrs. Giaquinto, and the one with the chickens is for Mrs. Wiederhorn. You know where they live, right?"

"Sure, sure," Frankie says.

"This bag here with the brains goes to Mrs. Morelli."

Frankie rolls his eyes and says, "What? She lose hers or something?"

I laugh. "Yeah, you think this is enough?"

All the Italian ladies around here are crazy for strange things like calf brains and tripe, which is cow stomach, and sweetbreads, which are animal parts I don't think anyone should be putting in their mouth. They like to fry the calf brains. Actually, it all tastes okay, as long as you don't think too hard about what you're eating.

"You two are a pair of regular comedians, aren't you?" Uncle Ralphie shakes his head. "Maybe you should go work for Jack Benny."

"Maybe we will," Frankie says.

Uncle Ralphie cuffs him lightly on the shoulder and says, "Where'd you get that smart mouth, kid?"

Frankie says, "From you," and we all laugh.

"Ralphie!" Aunt Fulvia hollers from up front.

"What now, *patanella mia*?" Uncle Ralphie shouts back.

"There's a fella up here saying he ordered a whole lamb, and I don't have any record of it," Aunt Fulvia says.

Uncle Ralphie groans and slaps his forehead. "I forgot all about Mr. Leckstein's lamb." He gives a long-suffering sigh. "You two get moving, and tell Mrs. Giaquinto I threw in some ham hocks for free."

As we pass Aunt Fulvia on the way out the front door, she calls after us, "You kids make sure you get paid, you hear me?"

We hop onto Frankie's bicycle. It has a basket in the front for the groceries. Pop-pop backed over my bicycle at the beginning of the summer. I guess I'm lucky he didn't run over me, too. I don't think he should even be driving, but just try telling him that.

The first stop is to see Mrs. Giaquinto, who we know as Ann Marie Harrison. Ann Marie used to date our cousin Benny, who's on Uncle Angelo's side of the family. Ann Marie and Benny would take Frankie and me to get ice cream. But then Benny went off to college last fall and Ann Marie married some other fella, and we haven't seen her around much lately.

I ring the doorbell, and after a moment the door opens a crack.

"Who is it?" Ann Marie asks in a nervous voice.

"It's Penny and Frankie," I say.

The door opens wider and we can see her. She's real pretty, with doe eyes like Elizabeth Taylor's.

"Hi, kids," Ann Marie says.

"How you doing, Ann Marie—I mean, Mrs. Giaquinto?" Frankie asks, blushing.

"You're getting tall, Frankie," she says. "How's Benny?"

"Good. He's studying to be an accountant, you know."

"Yes," she says, and there's something sad in her eyes.

"Uncle Ralphie put some ham hocks in the bag," I tell her.

"Who you talkin' to, Ann Marie?" a man's voice shouts in the background.

Ann Marie turns, and we see the purple bruise on her cheekbone. "It's just the grocery delivery, honey."

Frankie's mouth drops open, and before he can close it, the body of a huge, muscled man fills the doorway. The fella looks like a wrestler, and he's wearing a white undershirt and his eyes are blood-shot.

"What do you kids want?" he barks, and I can smell the whiskey on his breath.

Frankie steps in front of me and holds up the groceries. "Delivery."

The fella looks us up and down, then takes the bag.

"What're you waitin' for? A tip?" he growls.

"Thanks, kids," Ann Marie says, pressing some bills into our hands.

He shoves her inside and slams the door shut.

"'What're you waitin' for? A tip?'" Frankie mimics angrily.

I'm steering now; Frankie's sitting in back. "You see her cheek?" I ask.

Frankie doesn't say anything, but his arms tighten around my stomach.

Mrs. Wiederhorn's a widow, and when she opens the door she says, "Children! How are you? Are those for me? Why don't you come inside, and I'll get you some lemonade."

"Thanks," we say.

It's a small house, and every surface has a crocheted doily on it. She leads us into the kitchen, where a tired old cat stares at us from a cushion in the corner.

"Hi there, Miss Sniff," I say to the cat. "How old's Miss Sniff, anyhow?"

"Oh, very old, dear. Mr. Wiederhorn gave her to me for our fiftieth anniversary. Help yourselves," she says, and pushes a plate of cookies toward us.

We each take one. They're hard as rocks.

I politely sip my lemonade and pocket my cookie. It rubs against the lucky bean, which I always carry with me now.

Mrs. Wiederhorn is smiling at us. She doesn't seem to notice that she's still wearing her nightgown and it's lunchtime.

"How are the cookies, dears?" she asks.

"Real good," I say.

"If you're trying to kill someone," Frankie murmurs under his breath, and I have to bite my lip to keep from laughing.

"What was that, Frankie?" Mrs. Wiederhorn asks with a confused look.

"I said they're better than my own mother's," he says with a bright smile. Frankie's the best liar I know.

"Aren't you sweet," she says, pleased. "Take another."

"We don't want to ruin our dinner, ma'am," Frankie says quickly.

"Such good children," she says, and then turns to me. "How is your father, Penny?"

"Uh—uh," I stammer, "good, thanks."

"Your father is such a lovely man," she says. "He always brings me tomatoes from his garden."

Next to me Frankie groans, but I elbow him in

the ribs and just say, "He sure is."

Everyone knows that Mrs. Wiederhorn's been a little forgetful since her husband died. Well, a lot forgetful, I'd say, seeing as my father's been dead for years now.

She pays us and then offers us more cookies, but we say we have to go.

"We got more deliveries," Frankie tells her.

We wait until we're out of eyeshot of her house, and then we both throw our cookies into a bush.

Frankie says, "She's *pazza*." *Pazza* is Italian for "crazy."

"Yeah, but she's nice, right? I mean, the cookies and all?"

"I guess," he says.

"You ever been to Mrs. Morelli's house?" I ask as he pedals down the street.

"Nah, but I know Johnny Ferrara. He lives next to her."

The Morelli house looks sort of strange, like someone started to paint it and then gave up halfway through. There's a fence around the backyard with a sign that says BEWAR OF DOG. Looks like the Morellis can't spell in addition to not being able to paint.

"You got the brains?" Frankie asks as we walk to the front door.

"Do I ever!" I say, and grin.

The geraniums on the front porch are dead, and a chair with a broken seat leans against a post. Frankie rings the doorbell, and a dog starts barking from behind the fence. A big dog, judging from the barking.

"What do they need a guard dog for?" Frankie asks, looking around. "Nothing here worth stealing."

"Maybe we should come back later," I say nervously.

"Is she home or what?" Frankie says, standing on tiptoe and peering in through the window of the door. "I can't see a thing."

The gate to the fence is shaking like the dog is throwing his whole weight against it. I don't want to meet this dog.

"Frankie," I say, tugging his shirt, but he just ignores me and rings the bell again.

"Hey, Mrs. Morelli! Delivery from Falucci's!" he shouts.

There's a cracking sound. We turn and see the most enormous dog standing on what used to be the gate to the fence. It's a monster of a dog—Doberman–German shepherd, maybe a little rottweiler around the face. Whatever it is, it's mean and it starts growling when it sees Frankie and me standing there on the porch.

"Good dog," Frankie says as we slowly back away from the door. "See, we're leaving."

For a minute, it seems like the dog is going to back down, but then his whole body goes still, the way the principal, Mr. Shoup, gets before he whacks you with the ruler.

"Run, Frankie!" I shout.

We run for the bicycle like our lives depend on it, which they do. Frankie jumps on, and I grab on after him, and he starts pedaling. The dog doesn't seem to care that we're off his property, because he takes off after us, drool frothing at his mouth. This dog's out for blood!

"Faster, Frankie! Faster!" I shout as the dog lunges at my feet.

The dog is a bite away from me, and I'm thinking that the lucky bean that Uncle Dominic gave me is more of an unlucky bean when Frankie shouts, "Throw him the brains! Throw him the brains!"

I'm still holding the bag of calf brains.

"Here ya go, boy!" I shout, flinging the bag.

The last thing I see before we round the corner is the dog standing in the middle of the street gobbling up Mrs. Morelli's brains.

CHAPTER FOUR

A Man Who Can Fix a Toilet

I'm standing on the beach, my toes squishing in the sand.

The sky is blue, and the sun shining down is hot and bright. In front of me is the ocean, the waves rolling in, one after the other, and behind me is the boardwalk, with its rides and caramel corn and hot dogs. Overhead, gulls squawk down at me like the old Italian ladies Nonny plays cards with. All around me kids are running in and out of the shallows, dodging the waves. They shout and squeal, their cries mixing with the gulls and the crashing waves. But one voice stands out from all the others, calling to me.

"Penny!"

Out in the ocean, just past the next big wave, I

see a dark head bobbing in the water, hair slicked back like a seal's.

My father lifts his hand and waves.

I wade out into the water, and when it reaches my chest, I dive into an oncoming wave. I'm a good swimmer. I learned how to swim at the lake we go to every summer. But for some reason, the farther I swim, the farther away my father seems to be, until he is just a speck on the horizon.

"Penny," my father calls to me, his voice distant now.

A wave rises from the ocean and comes crashing down, dragging me under.

His voice rings through the water: "Penny!"

I fight my way up to the surface, but when I blink my eyes open, I'm not in the ocean. There's no sand, no blue sky, no waves.

I'm lying in my bed, the sheets kicked off. Water is pouring down through the ceiling, and it doesn't smell at all like seawater.

"Pop-pop," I yell. "The toilet's leaking again!"

"Give me the other wrench," Pop-pop says, banging around on his hands and knees on the black-and-white-tiled bathroom floor.

"Which one?" I ask, looking in his mess of a

toolbox. There are at least five wrenches.

"What?"

"Which wrench?" I say loudly.

"The other one," he says. "The other one!"

I pick one out and hand it to him.

"Useless," he grumbles, and starts smacking it on the toilet.

The toilet is always breaking, and lucky for me, it's right over my bed. Pop-pop refuses to hire a plumber. He always says, "Any man worth his salt can fix a toilet."

Me-me is in the kitchen when I go downstairs.

"Did he fix it?" she asks.

I shake my head.

"That man is so stubborn," she says under her breath. "I swear, he'd sit on the *Titanic* while it was sinking just because he wouldn't want to give up his seat."

There's a loud bang followed by a curse, and we both look up.

Me-me shakes her head. "I'd better go up there before he tears apart the whole bathroom. Go see if the milk has been delivered yet."

Me-me likes to put the top cream from the milk into her coffee, and after dealing with Pop-pop, she's going to need some coffee.

I go out to the porch just in time to see Mr.

Mulligan, the milkman, coming up the walk carrying two bottles of milk.

"Hi, Mr. Mulligan," I say.

"Hi, Penny," he says back. "I think we're in for a hot one today."

Mr. Mulligan is going bald and only has a tuft of red hair left, like Woody Woodpecker. He's from an Irish family and he's got real pale skin. We get a lot of deliverymen coming here—milk, bread, vegetables—but Mr. Mulligan's the nicest. He's got a good sense of humor.

"Let's see, you have four bottles of milk, right?" he asks, which is what he always asks. It's sort of a joke with us, because we get the same thing every week. Not very exciting, but there it is.

"Four bottles," I say.

"You a big milk drinker?" he asks.

"I hate milk," I say. "But Me-me makes me drink it."

He laughs. "See you next week."

After fixing the toilet, Pop-pop announces that we're going to paint Me-me's desk. Lately, Pop-pop's been painting all the furniture in the house black. Me-me thinks our old furniture will look nicer with black lacquer paint. She got the idea from her friend Mrs. Hart, who's painted all her furniture and woodwork with black lacquer paint and says it's very stylish. I can't say that I like it very much. You kind of feel like you're in a funeral parlor.

"Ready for some fancy painting?" Pop-pop asks.

We drag Me-me's desk out to the summer porch. First we sand the desk so that the paint will take, and then we start painting. It's not exactly the best day to be painting; it's about a hundred degrees out. The whole time we paint, Pop-pop keeps up a running commentary on how I'm doing everything wrong.

"You're using too much paint," he'll say, or "Hold the brush *this* way." His favorite is "Don't they teach you anything in that school of yours?"

Scarlett O'Hara is sitting on the porch, looking out at the squirrels in the backyard. All at once a large puddle forms at her feet.

"Scarlett!" I say, but it's too late. She blinks up at me and wags her tail.

"Out of here, mutt," Pop-pop says, holding the door open and glaring at Scarlett O'Hara.

"Go on, Scarlett," I say, and she bolts out after a squirrel.

Scarlett loves chasing other animals. Anytime she senses another creature, she goes after it. Once she chased a chipmunk all around the house before scaring it into running up the chimney, which Mother didn't think was very clever but I thought was pretty funny, especially when the chipmunk came back down all covered in soot and ran around the parlor.

"Pop-pop," I ask, "do you think something's wrong with Scarlett O'Hara?"

"She's an old dog," he says.

Scarlett O'Hara's almost fifteen, which I guess is old in dog years, although she sure doesn't act old. My father gave my mother Scarlett O'Hara when she was just a puppy, but now she's my dog. Mother says that when I was a baby, Scarlett would bark whenever I cried.

"What does that have to do with tinkling on the floor?" I ask.

He groans and stands up. "When you get old, sometimes your innards stop working the way they should."

"Does that mean she's going to die?"

"We're all going to die," he says. "I'm planning on dropping dead next week. That way I don't have to wear a necktie to that social with your grand-mother."

We paint together for a while, and then Me-me comes out to the porch with meat loaf sandwiches and lemonade. I don't like meat loaf to begin with, and Me-me's meat loaf is dry and crusty. Pop-pop starts right in on his sandwich, but when I try to take a bite of mine, my stomach gives a little flip. All this talk of dying is getting to me. Either that or it's the meat loaf. It's hard to say.

I pull the lucky bean out of my pocket. It doesn't look very lucky. I think of my dream. Would my father have died if he'd had this bean? I know he got sick and was taken to the hospital and died there, but no one on either side of the family ever really talks about what was wrong with him.

"Pop-pop, what did my father die from?" I ask.

"What? What?" he sputters.

"I just thought you might know, is all."

"How would I know?" he asks with a huff. "Do I look like a doctor?"

Before I can say anything, the squirrel Scarlett O'Hara's been chasing runs in through the open screen door and starts racing around the enclosed porch, with Scarlett right behind it. Scarlett streaks by the desk, smearing black paint all along her side.

"Penny, get that blasted dog out of here!" Pop-pop hollers.

"Scarlett O'Hara," I call. I lunge for her, but she outmaneuvers me, and my foot catches in the rug.

And that's when I go tumbling headfirst right into the can of paint.

"Oh, Penny," Me-me says with a sigh.

We're in the upstairs bathroom, hers and Pop-pop's. Leaky toilet aside, I've always liked it better. It's bigger than mine and Mother's. The bathtub has great big claw feet and it's deep, so deep that you can almost disappear in it when there are bubbles.

Me-me's looking over my shoulder into the mirror on the wall. One chunk of my hair has a swipe of black paint on it that even the turpentine won't take out. Me-me is going to shave down Scarlett O'Hara where she got paint on her fur, but she doesn't know what to do with me.

"You have such pretty hair," she says, touching my curls. "Your mother's hair looked the same way when she was a girl."

It was burned by a perm? I want to say. Instead, I say, "Maybe I can try soaking it for a while."

She runs a big bath, pours in some bubbles, and I slip out of my clothes and get into the tub, leaning back against the high white rim. I close my eyes as Me-me soaps up my hair, her fingers strong. It feels wonderful.

"Can we make ice cream tonight?" I ask. "Butter pecan?"

I love pecans. I could eat pecans on anything— ice cream, cookies, hot dogs, you name it.

"I don't see why not," Me-me says.

Me-me is like this: Sometimes she's tough as old nails and sometimes she's a real softy.

"You know," Me-me says, "when we lived in Key West, we made sugar-apple ice cream. That was always my favorite. Can you imagine when I learned there were no sugar-apple trees up north? It almost broke my heart."

Me-me grew up in Key West, Florida. Pop-pop met her when he was in the army. Me-me's always talking about how she misses Key West, and Pop-pop always says that it was the worst place he ever lived, nothing but scorpions, and that he couldn't wait to get back to New Jersey.

"Is the paint coming out?" I ask hopefully.

"I'm sorry, Penny," she says.

I get out of the tub and put a towel on and stand still while Me-me cuts. When she's done, it looks like someone was drawing me and then erased part out. I sure hope it grows back fast.

Maybe it's because I've been thinking about my father all day, but I just blurt out, "Do I look like my father?"

Me-me hesitates and then says, "You look like him around the eyes. You have his eyes."

"I do?"

"Yes," she says finally. "Your father had beautiful eyes."

My bedroom was once a closet, so I guess you could say it's cozy.

It wasn't planned that way. My mother and father bought this house when they were first married. But then he died and my mother needed help with me, so Me-me and Pop-pop sold their own house and moved in here. They converted the upstairs into their half and the downstairs into ours. My room used to be the pantry, and on a damp day it still smells like cinnamon.

All that fits in my room is a bed and a small dressing table. I keep my clothes in a closet in Mother's room. I got to decorate the room myself, and at the time I really liked poodles, so there's poodle wallpaper and a poodle headboard and the lamp has a poodle base. I even have a matching poodle bedspread that Me-me made. Lately I've been thinking of asking Mother if I can redecorate. I'm a little tired of the poodles.

But now as I lie in my bed, I'm thinking maybe I should ask if I can get a window while I'm at it. It's not too bad in the winter, but on nights like this, it's just awful. It's hot as an oven. Even though I'm wearing the thinnest cotton pajama set I have, I'm still sweating up a storm. The fan that's propped in the doorway isn't helping one bit. Me-me's the only one not bothered by hot nights like this.

Finally I give up and grab my pillow and head out to the summer porch. It's still hot, but at least there's a stingy breeze here. Pop-pop's already on the wicker couch, snoring away, so I take the swing. Scarlett O'Hara must have forgiven him for the paint job, because she's curled up behind his knees. She looks sort of naked and embarrassed without her hair. I know just how she feels.

After Me-me butchered my hair, I went over to see Frankie. I don't see Frankie as much during the school year because he goes to Catholic school and I go to public school. But Frankie's pretty much my best friend. Not that I have a lot of friends lately, thanks to Veronica Goodman. I ran into her outside the Sweete Shoppe with a bunch of other girls from school. She burst out laughing when she saw my horrible hair.

"That the new style, Penny?" she asked. The other girls laughed too.

I wanted to disappear right into the ground.

Veronica and I used to be friends. In fact, we were good friends until last fall, when everything changed. See, my uncle Ralphie owns the building next to Falucci's Market, and he rents it out. Veronica's father wanted to rent the space to put in a shoe store, but Uncle Ralphie rented it to someone else. Uncle Ralphie said it wasn't personal; the fella he rented it to could pay more. But I guess Mr. Goodman didn't see it that way, because he got angry and went and called my Uncle Ralphie some bad names for being Italian. Ever since that happened, Veronica has been mean to me, and most of the other girls have ignored me. Veronica's pretty popular.

The scent of black paint swirls in my nose as I lie there looking out at the dark night. These are the times I think about my father the most. What is he doing up there in Heaven? Is he just sitting on a cloud, or is he listening to Bing Crosby? Is he dancing the jitterbug? Eating an ice cream sundae?

If I could ask Mother one question about my father, it would be what he thought of me. Did he think I was funny? Or smart? Did he love me?

I hear a soft step and look up to see my mother standing there wearing a nice dress and hat. Her cheeks are glowing. She went out to dinner and to play bridge with her friend Connie. They've been going out together a lot lately, and I think it's good for her. She seems happier.

"Too hot in your room?" she whispers.

I nod. "Pop-pop beat me to the couch."

"He's fast for an old fella, huh?" she says with a laugh. "Scoot over."

She sits down, unpins her hat, and then blinks as she takes in my head. "What happened to your hair?"

"I got paint on it," I say. Scarlett O'Hara whimpers as if she doesn't like to be left out, and I say, "Scarlett O'Hara did, too."

My mother just shakes her head. "How was dinner?"

"Beef Stroganoff." I wrinkle my nose. "There's *lots* of leftovers."

She laughs. "No, thank you."

"We made ice cream," I tell her. "Butter pecan. Want some?"

"Now that I'll take," she says, and I go inside and get her a bowl.

She takes a spoonful and makes an appreciative sound.

"Did you have fun with Connie?" I ask.

"I had a lovely time," she says, and smiles to herself.

My mother leans against me and kicks the floor, which sets the swing in motion. We stare out at the night, the fireflies dancing in the trees. Pop-pop snorts in his sleep and turns over. There's a small hissing sound, and Scarlett O'Hara whimpers and jumps off the couch and trots over to us.

"Mother," I whisper, wrinkling my nose.

"Yes?" she says.

"What's that smell?"

"I think it's Pop-pop," she whispers back, and we both giggle.

CHAPTER FIVE

The Luckiest Fella Ever

The first difference between Me-me's kitchen and my Italian grandmother's is the smell. My grandmother Falucci's kitchen smells delicious: like basil and tomatoes and garlic. It makes your mouth water.

The second difference is that Nonny's kitchen is downstairs in the basement. There's a stove and a refrigerator and a big sink and a wooden cutting table and pots and pans.

In the corner is a wringer washing machine. It's usually my job to help with the laundry if I'm around, same as at my house.

There's a regular modern kitchen upstairs that my aunt Gina uses. Uncle Paulie bought the house from my grandmother, but she still lives here and everyone still calls it her house. Nonny doesn't approve of the way Aunt Gina cooks and so she demanded a kitchen of her own in the basement. At first Uncle Paulie said no, but then he put one in "to keep the peace." Uncle Paulie spends a lot of time keeping the peace between the women in his life.

"I should've been a diplomat," he always says, shaking his head. "Least I'd be getting paid."

When I walk down the rickety basement stairs, Nonny's back is to me. She's tiny, maybe eighty pounds, and her legs are like two thin black-stockinged toothpicks poking out from underneath her black dress. I've never actually seen her in anything but black. Even her winter coat is black Persian lamb.

"Hi, Nonny," I say. *Nonna* is Italian for "grandmother." The story goes that I couldn't say *Nonna* when I was little, so I called her Nonny, and it just sort of stuck. Now everyone calls her that.

Nonny turns around, takes one look at me, and bursts into tears.

I sigh. I'm used to it, I guess. She cries every time she sees me.

My father, Alfredo, who everyone called Freddy, was her favorite, the firstborn son. He was the first person in the family to go to college, and he became a newspaper writer. Everyone was so proud of him, especially Nonny. His death was the worst thing that ever happened to the family. A real tragedy. Which is why Nonny wears black and cries every time she sees me.

"Tesoro mio," Nonny says, wiping away her tears with a black lace handkerchief. She calls me *tesoro mio,* which means "my treasure." Nonny doesn't speak English very well.

I take my usual spot on the stool by the table, and she pushes a plate at me and says in her thick Italian accent, "Too skinny. Eat. Eat."

Sitting on the plate is something Nonny calls *pastiera,* a dish made with spaghetti and eggs and cheese and black pepper that's baked and served cold. It's one of my favorites, so Nonny cooks it all the time for me.

I watch as her small, gnarled fingers knead dough for fresh macaroni. All the Italian women in my family make their own macaroni. Nonny carefully rolls out the dough and then takes a sharp knife and cuts it into long strips and hangs it to dry on a wooden rack. Sometimes she lets me help her make it.

Nonny wipes her hands on her apron. "We see your papa now, yes?" She says this like it's a question, but I know it's not.

Uncle Paulie is already waiting for us in the upstairs hallway.

"There's my ladies," Uncle Paulie says with a broad smile.

My uncle Paulie's a big, round fella. Probably because he has to eat two dinners every night: one cooked by Aunt Gina and one cooked by Nonny.

Nonny ties a black lace scarf around her head.

"Paolo," she says, and points to her gloves. Paolo is Paulie's name in Italian.

"Here ya go, Ma," Uncle Paulie says, handing her the black gloves.

"Freddy," Nonny says, waving at the wall in the hallway where there's a shrine to my dead father. There's a dozen photographs of him: at his First Holy Communion; at his graduation from high school; one with his arm around Uncle Dominic when they were young, the two of them grinning like they've got some big secret.

"Your father was a great man, Penny. Real good fella. Best brother ever," Uncle Paulie says.

I've heard this a million times. And I know the next part, too.

Nonny starts crying. "My Freddy good boy."

"That's right," Uncle Paulie says, a fat tear rolling down his cheek.

"Regular party in here," a voice says from the top of the stairs.

It's Aunt Gina. She's wearing a white silk top with a fitted skirt and holding a cigarette. With her bleached-blond hair, she looks glamorous, like Marilyn Monroe.

"Hi, Aunt Gina," I say.

"Hi, doll," she says, walking down the steps, eyeing Nonny standing by the door with her scarf and gloves. "Honey, I thought you said you were taking me shopping today."

"Paolo," Nonny says.

Uncle Paulie lowers his voice. "I gotta take Ma to see Freddy."

"The cemetery," Aunt Gina says, her voice dry.

Uncle Paulie nods uncomfortably.

"Sounds like a real swell time," Aunt Gina says, tapping her cigarette.

Nonny mutters something in Italian and my eyes widen. I know that curse word.

"What's that, Mother Falucci?" Aunt Gina asks loudly.

Aunt Gina doesn't know much Italian, and she always thinks that Nonny is trying to insult her, which is probably true because Nonny doesn't like Aunt Gina. I personally think Uncle Paulie is going bald trying to survive in a house with two women who don't get along.

Frankie walks in the front door.

"Francuccio," Nonny says, and kisses him on both cheeks and hugs him tight until he wiggles free. *Francuccio* means "little Frankie."

"Where's everybody going?" he asks, taking in the scene.

"The cemetery," I whisper.

"Oh, swell!" Frankie says loudly. "I love the cemetery!"

Aunt Gina taps her foot.

"Ready, Ma?" Uncle Paulie says nervously. "We better get going."

Aunt Gina glares at Uncle Paulie, but he takes Nonny by the elbow and practically shoves her out the door, saying, "See ya later, honey."

As the screen door slams behind us, Aunt Gina shouts, "I tell you, the only way to get someone to pay attention to you in this family is by dying!"

"Penny, look at this one," Frankie says in an excited voice, pointing at an old gravestone that looks like it's going to fall over any minute. "It's got a skull on it. Whaddya think?"

"Could be," I say.

"Definitely," he says. "Get a load of the name. *Howard Pfeiffer*. That's a criminal's name if I ever heard one."

Frankie likes coming to the cemetery because he heard there are a lot of criminals buried here. See, he reads crime comic books, and he thinks that they're true. His favorite is *Crime Does Not Pay*. He won't read real books, but he'll read comic books.

Some of the graves have patriotic red, white, and blue flags stuck on them. These are the graves of fallen soldiers. A lot of men from our town were killed in the world wars.

My father's gravestone is marble, imported all the way from Italy, where we have lots of relatives. Uncle Nunzio had it made by a master carver, some cousin who does everyone's stones. It's the only gravestone with an Italian name in the whole row.

ALFREDO CHRISTOPHER FALUCCI

There's a Catholic cemetery across the street, and that's where my grandfather Falucci is buried. My father's buried here because my mother hadn't converted to Catholicism by the time he died, so they weren't allowed to bury him in the Catholic cemetery. Nonny's still upset about that.

"How's it going, Freddy?" Uncle Paulie says to the ground. Uncle Paulie always talks like my father's going to crawl right out of his grave and go off and smoke a cigar with him.

Nonny gets down on her knees and starts picking weeds, although it's already the neatest grave in the entire cemetery. The groundskeeper, an old skinny fella named Lou, takes extra special care of my father's plot. Uncle Ralphie sends him a ham at Christmas. Not to mention we're here just about every week. To be honest, I hate it. I just do it because it makes Nonny happy.

"Real nice day for a visit, huh, Penny?" Uncle Paulie says, puffing away on a cigar. I guess dead people don't mind the smell.

But Uncle Paulie's right. It's a perfect day, not too hot, and I start thinking that maybe there are worse ways of passing time than being here in Shady Grove Cemetery. It's a peaceful cemetery, with trees everywhere. Not a bad place to be dead, if you ask me.

My father's grave is sandwiched between Stuart Brandt, a young soldier, and Cora Lamb, a girl who died when she was nine. Stuart's stone says:

STUART BRANDT
Valiant Soldier and Beloved Son
He Gave His Life for Our Freedom
March 19, 1923–June 6, 1944

Cora has a marble sculpture on her grave—a baby angel with short stubby wings. One time when we were visiting my father's grave, I met Cora Lamb's mother. She was an old lady with gray hair. I asked her how Cora died.

"The flu," said Mrs. Lamb.

I think about Cora Lamb sometimes. Did she like butter pecan ice cream and read the funny pages? Did she fight with her mother about what dress to wear? Did she have a favorite toy? A fancy doll? See, I think it's important to know someone's story.

My uncles tell me stories about my father all the time. Uncle Dominic likes to tell the story of how he and my father went into New York City when they were just teenagers and got pickpocketed. So my father stood on the corner of Forty-second Street and Broadway and sang every Bing Crosby song he knew until they made enough money for the train fare home. Uncle Paulie always tells the one about how my father once bet twenty dollars on a pony named Lucky Duck at the racetrack and won and bought everyone in their section a bag of peanuts.

My grandmother is crying.

"Freddy," Nonny says, patting the stone. "So wrong, what happen to my boy. Those bad men. *Non è giusto. Non è giusto.*"

"What's she talking about?" I ask Uncle Paulie. "What bad men?"

Uncle Paulie clears his throat. "Uh, the doctors who treated him. She blames them for what happened. You know how she is about hospitals."

Nonny hates hospitals. She cut her finger once chopping garlic and refused to go to the hospital. Everyone thought she was gonna lose the finger, but she didn't.

"What'd my father die from, anyway, Uncle Paulie?" I ask.

"Pneumonia," he says quickly. "Real bad case of pneumonia."

Frankie sidles up to us. "Pneumonia? That's a boring way to die. How about a shot to the head? Or maybe knifed in a back alley?"

"Aw, shut up, kid," Uncle Paulie says. "Last time I bring you here."

If my Italian family didn't talk about my father, I wouldn't know a thing, because my mother won't tell me anything. All she's ever said is that he liked

Bing Crosby, and honestly, what does that tell you about a person? Nothing, that's what.

There's a box under my mother's bed that I found by accident. Scarlett O'Hara has a habit of stealing my socks and then hiding them, usually under beds, so I was looking for a sock when I found a pink department-store box. There wasn't much in it—a few cards, a dried corsage, some shells, a bunch of photographs. One of the photographs was of my mother when she was younger, maybe twenty. She was wearing a bathing suit on the beach and laughing at the camera. She looked like a completely different person, so happy and carefree.

At the very bottom of the box was a picture postcard from Atlantic City. It was of a hotel, the Chalfonte–Haddon Hall, "in the very center of things on the Beach and Boardwalk." The note was in my mother's handwriting:

Dear Mother and Daddy,
Here we are on our honeymoon and having a grand time. Our room is beautiful and it looks out to the ocean. The weather is clear and cool and our appetites are large.
Love to all,
Ellie and Freddy

Scribbled beneath this in my father's handwriting was a little note that said:

I am the luckiest fella ever.

I've never told anyone about the postcard—not even Frankie, and I tell him everything.

"We better start back," Uncle Paulie says, helping Nonny up.

As we drive down Heavenly Lane of Shady Grove Cemetery, I'm proud that my father was the clever brother who sang for the train fare and the swell fella who bought peanuts for everybody after his pony won.

But more than just about anything in the whole wide world, it's the man who wrote "I am the luckiest fella ever" on that postcard who I wish I could've met.

CHAPTER SIX

Uncles, Uncles Everywhere

My mother always says that even though my father's family is full of men, don't be fooled. It's the women who really run things.

It's Sunday, and that means dinner at Nonny's house. On Saturdays I have dinner at home, which is usually a dry pot roast and burned potatoes because Me-me leaves it in too long. I don't know when this started, me going over to my father's family on Sundays; it's been this way forever. And it's always just me, never my mother or Me-me or Pop-pop.

My Italian family starts their dinner in the afternoon, so I go over after lunchtime. Everyone's sitting in the upstairs kitchen around the table and the room smells like lemons. They put the lemons in the decanters of homemade Chianti. An Italian opera's playing on the record player. My Italian family is crazy about opera music.

All the uncles are here—Uncle Paulie, Uncle Ralphie, Uncle Nunzio, who's married to Aunt Rosa and lives next door in a house that has two stone lions guarding the front door, and Frankie's dad, Uncle Angelo. They're my real uncles. Nonny had six kids—my father, Uncle Dominic, Uncle Paulie, Aunt Teresa, Uncle Ralphie, and Aunt Rosa. Then there's my father's cousins, who Frankie and me still call our uncles. There's Uncle Sally, whose real name is Salvatore, and Uncle Chick, who's in the ironworks business, and Uncle Louis, who raises fig trees in his backyard, and my other uncle Louis, who everyone calls Little Louis because he's younger—even though he weighs three hundred pounds and isn't exactly little; in fact, I think he could stand to go on a diet. Pretty much everyone is related somehow. I don't think anyone's not Italian, except me, and even I'm half.

It's times like these that I wish I understood Italian. But they won't teach it to any of us kids because they say it's our job to speak English and be good Americans.

Aunt Gina says the reason they don't want us to learn Italian is that during World War II, Italy was on the wrong side, with Germany and Japan, and so the Italians who were in America got in trouble for it. She says that even Joe DiMaggio's father had problems, and if Joe DiMaggio's pop can get in trouble, you got to watch it, and this is why my relatives always speak English in public. But Frankie thinks the real reason they don't want us to know Italian is so that they can have secret conversations. Frankie and me know all the good curse words anyway.

"There's our golden girl," Uncle Nunzio says. He's wearing a real nice suit, charcoal gray with a thin pinstripe. It looks like something a Hollywood movie star would wear.

Uncle Nunzio owns a clothing factory, which is probably why he's such a snappy dresser. He's not handsome like Uncle Dominic, but there's something about him. He has this way of looking at you, like he's looking right into your soul. I don't think too many people cross Uncle Nunzio.

"Hi, Uncle Nunzio," I say.

"How are you, sweetheart?" he asks.

"Good."

He gestures to a plate of fresh Italian pastries. "Eat something."

"Thanks," I say, and pick up a *sfogliatella*. *Sfogliatelle* are pastry with ricotta cheese inside. It sounds funny but they're really good.

Aunt Gina walks in with Aunt Rosa, who likes to pinch me on the cheeks, and Aunt Teresa, who always looks worn-out, and our cousin Sister Laura, who's a nun.

This is how it is here: people coming and going. There's always a pot of something bubbling on the stove, a glass of Chianti being poured, macaroni in the oven. They think nothing of playing Italian card games like *scopa* or *briscola* until two in the morning. I don't think my mother has ever even been up until two in the morning, let alone had someone arrive at midnight to join a game.

I slip away and go look for Uncle Dominic. He doesn't like big gatherings, even if it is family, and he usually hides out in his car. The car's empty, so I go around back and find him with the girls, which is what he calls his dogs.

As long as I've known him, Uncle Dominic's had dogs, and they're always dachshunds. I call them wiener dogs because they look like the wieners you get at the boardwalk. He's got two right now, Queenie V and Queenie VI. Queenies I, II, III, and IV are dead and buried somewhere in the backyard. He names the boy dogs King, but there've only been two Kings so far. A couple of years ago Uncle Dominic built the dogs a pen so that they can tear around and play and not get run over in the street, which is what happened to the dead Queenies and the Kings, too.

When I get to the pens, Uncle Dominic's talking to one of the dogs.

"How's my favorite girl?" he's saying, like the dog is a regular person. Uncle Dominic talks to the dogs a lot, and he cooks special for them. When you come right down to it, I think he prefers them to people. He says dogs are nicer. Also, they don't care if he wears his slippers.

Nonny loves the Queenies too. She's always spraying the fancy perfume Uncle Paulie buys her, Tabu, on them. She speaks to them in Italian, and they're probably the only dogs I know that can understand two languages.

"I thought I was your favorite girl," I say.

He looks startled for a minute and then, realizing it's just me, relaxes.

"Hi, Princess."

"Taught them any new tricks?"

Uncle Dominic says wiener dogs are real smart. I'm not too sure about this, though. They can't be that smart if they're always chasing cars and getting run over.

"I'm working on something," he says. "I'll show you when it's ready."

Aunt Rosa pokes her head out the door, the sun

catching in her thick, dark hair. "What are you two up to out here?"

She's my father's youngest sister, the baby of the family. When she was a teenager, she was always running away to New York City. My uncles would have to go and find her and bring her home. The story goes that her brothers got tired of tracking her down and so they sent their friend Nunzio to go get her, and when he brought her back, they were engaged. Uncle Nunzio must be some kind of a smooth talker.

"Just playing with the Queenies," I say.

"Well, come on in. Dinner's ready," she says.

"Go on," Uncle Dominic says. He never takes meals with us, which, believe me, is saying something in an Italian family. He's like a shadow; he just drifts in and out with nobody paying much attention to him, except maybe me.

Pretty soon I'm sitting at the long dining room table with the lacy tablecloth that Nonny made herself. We're all crammed in and everyone's talking at once and laughing and arguing and it's real loud.

Baby Enrico, who's Aunt Rosa's baby, waddles over to my chair. He's almost two and is real mischievous. But he's got the best smile that you've ever seen.

He holds his arms up to me and says, "Carry you! Carry you!"

What he's trying to say is "Carry me!" but he thinks it's "Carry you!" since people ask him, "You want me to carry you?"

"Come here," I say, and pick him up and put him on my lap. He fishes around on my plate, takes a piece of bread and gnaws on it, and then tries to stick it in my mouth.

"Eat!" he orders. He's Italian already.

Frankie and me used to get a lot of attention until all the baby cousins started showing up. In addition to Enrico there's Uncle Ralphie and Aunt Fulvia's baby, Gloria, and Frankie's baby brother, Michael, and Aunt Rosa's pregnant again. I like the baby cousins, especially Enrico, but I hate changing smelly diapers.

Dinner is a big production here, and it takes hours. We usually start off with some soup, and then we have macaroni, and then some meat, like breast of veal or *braciole,* which is braised beef rolls, with vegetables and potatoes. After that there's salad, just lettuce with oil and vinegar, no tomatoes or anything else. Then there's a break, and all the men go drink anisette in the parlor or play bocce ball in the backyard while the women sit around eating raw fennel. Then comes coffee and nuts and fruit and cordials. After that, we'll sometimes have a snack.

I start in on the soup, which has escarole and bits of egg. The food I eat here is completely different than at home. Here, food is everything. They even call the food by different names. They call pasta "macaroni." At home we say it's tomato sauce, and here they call it gravy.

"Why don't you come down to the factory, Penny?" Uncle Nunzio says to me. "Pick out your fall coat. The new styles are in."

I get a new coat every year from Uncle Nunzio. I also get a lot of other clothes—muffs and hats and matching skirts and jackets. I never have to shop in stores like regular people. I just tell Uncle Nunzio what I like, and he has one of the ladies sew it up for me.

"Okay," I say. "Thanks."

Nonny walks into the room, carrying a huge casserole dish. Nonny and my aunts cook enough to feed an army. "Just in case people show up" is what they always say.

Today she's made lasagna, which is my favorite.

"Looks good," I say as she puts a large portion on my plate. She always puts too much on my plate and gets upset when I don't eat it all. It doesn't matter how much I eat: I can never eat enough to make her happy.

After dinner the uncles break out their instruments and start playing. There's a trumpet, a mandolin, a violin, and the piano. They're like their own band. Soon everyone's singing and dancing and loud, and it's a regular party.

It's nearly six o'clock by the time I leave. Before I go, everyone kisses me good-bye on both cheeks, something we never do in my family. They also slip money into my hands, rolled-up one-dollar bills. I kind of like this tradition.

"I'll drive you home," Uncle Dominic says. I'm perfectly capable of walking home by myself, but he never lets me. He's almost as bad as my mother.

At my house he idles at the curb, watching to make sure I get in okay. I give him a little wave. I go into the parlor, and for a moment I think everybody's asleep or something. But they're in the dining room, eating dinner.

They're so quiet, I hardly know they're there.

The next morning I borrow Frankie's bike and go to Uncle Nunzio's factory.

The clothing factory is on the other side of

town. It's a big brick building that looks just like every other big brick building. During the war the factory made uniforms for the military, but now it makes regular clothes, mostly awfully nice wool coats. You can hear the sewing machines buzzing even before you go in.

Carolina, Uncle Nunzio's secretary, is sitting at her desk outside his office. She's wearing a stylish suit with a fake-flower corsage.

"Hi, hon. Your uncle's on the phone. He'll be done in a minute," she says.

I sit on a bench to wait. It's hot inside, real hot, even with the fans going, and I feel sorry for all the ladies at their sewing machines, row after row, sweating away. Most of them are from Italy.

"You want a butterscotch?" Carolina asks, holding out a tin.

"Sure," I say, taking one.

"How's your mother?" she asks. She and my mom went to school together.

"She's good, thanks."

"You look more like her every day," she says.

"I sure hope she didn't have this hairdo when she was my age."

Carolina laughs. "Oh, your mother could've pulled off that hairdo. She was the most daring girl I knew."

"My mother was daring? Honest to goodness?" I can't picture my mom like this at all. She won't go out of the house without an umbrella and scarf even on a clear day.

"Would I lie to you?" Carolina says with a laugh. "Our senior year, she helped steal our school rival's mascot, a goat."

"A goat!"

The door to the office opens, and Uncle Nunzio is standing there.

"It's the little princess," he says with a broad smile.

"Hi, Uncle Nunzio," I say.

"Ask Alberto to come in for a minute, eh, Carolina?" Uncle Nunzio says.

A short elderly man with gray hair and a tape measure hanging around his neck comes into the office. Alberto's been my uncle's tailor forever.

"Alberto," Uncle Nunzio says, "Penny needs a new coat."

"*Bellissima,*" he says to me, which I know means "most beautiful girl" in Italian.

Alberto leads me out of the office and over to a workroom in the factory where the coats are stored. There are all sorts of coats—coats with shiny buttons and fur collars and matching gloves and everything. I spot a nubby wool coat that's cranberry red with a rabbit-fur collar and rabbit fur around the wrists. It has a matching muff and hat.

"That one, please," I say.

Alberto has me try it on, but it's a little long in the sleeves. He takes the coat over to a sewing machine and fixes it while I wait.

Uncle Nunzio is in his office looking at some papers when I come in, the coat over my arm.

"Got one?" he asks, looking up.

"Yeah," I say, holding up the coat. "Thanks."

"You take the muff, too?"

I shake my head. "I got the hat."

"Take the muff," he says. "It's rabbit. The best."

He goes to the door and calls to Carolina, "Get Penny the muff, okay?"

"You got it, Mr. Rosati," she says.

"What about your mother?" he asks me. "She need a new coat?"

"Sure," I say, although I know she doesn't like gifts from my father's family for some reason. Maybe she's worried about getting more lamb's eyes.

We go back to the coat room. He waves at a rack in the corner.

"Pick something out," he says.

I look through the coats. They're all so beautiful, trimmed in mink and rabbit and lynx. But it's the reddish fox stole that catches my eye. It will go with my mother's hair, and it's something she would never pick out for herself in a hundred years. The fur gleams in the dim light, and the little teeth of the fox are bared and angry-looking, like it's not too happy to be a stole.

The coat and muff and hat go in the basket of the bike, but I wear the fox stole draped around my neck the whole way home, feeling like a movie star. I imagine my mother wearing it, looking glamorous, although I'm not sure where she would go. Usually she spends her Friday nights listening to the radio with me and Pop-pop and Me-me.

When I was younger, she used to date. They were always good-looking fellas, but they never came back after she introduced them to me. I guess they didn't want kids. Mother hasn't dated in a long time, but I keep hoping that maybe she and Uncle Dominic will get together. He's handsome and he already likes me and I'm sure I could work on the living in the car and get him to wear a pair of shoes.

When I get home, Frankie's waiting on the front porch.

"Couldn't take hearing the baby cry no more," he tells me. Baby Michael's real colicky, and I guess no one's been getting much sleep at Frankie's house these days.

He sees the fur stole and asks, "That your fancy new coat?" It irritates Frankie that the uncles are always giving me presents, even though he knows it's because my father is dead and everybody feels sorry for me.

"It's not for me. It's for Mother," I say. "This one's for me." I hold up the red coat.

"'Little princess,'" he mimics. "You'll look like Red Riding Hood in that getup."

"Aw, shut up, Frankie," I say.

Frankie follows me into the house. It's dark and quiet.

"Me-me? Pop-pop?" I call out, and then I find the note on the table.

Penny,
Gone shopping. Put the tuna casserole in the oven at 4:30.
Love, Me-me

"You want to stay over for dinner tonight? Me-me made a tuna casserole," I tell Frankie.

He considers it and then shakes his head. "Nah, I want to survive the summer."

Frankie's brought his baseball mitts, so we go out to the backyard. He wants to practice fielding, and he has me throw him ground balls. After a bunch of grounders, I throw the ball high in the air.

"I tell ya, it's a crying shame, you being a girl," he says. "That arm of yours is like a cannon."

Frankie's always trying to get me to play on his team. Sometimes I do if they don't have enough boys.

"I mean it," Frankie says. "You got talent. Must be Uncle Dom's blood."

"Long as I don't end up living in a car," I say.

"If he was still playing ball, he wouldn't be living in the car," he says.

"Why do you think he quit, anyway?" I ask.

"Beats me," he says. "Maybe he wasn't good enough. I gotta use the can."

"I gotta use the can" is his favorite expression. He heard Benny say it, and now he says it every chance he can get. It sounds a lot ruder than "tinkle."

After a while I get to wondering where Frankie has wandered to. I walk into the house and hear the sound of water leaking. I go into my bedroom and look up and see water coming through the ceiling. By the time I get to the upstairs bathroom, Frankie's already put every towel on the floor and water's still coming out of the toilet.

"What did you do?" I demand.

"Nothing!" he says.

"Why'd you use this bathroom?"

"I don't know. I like it. It's bigger," he says.

"You gotta make it stop!" I say.

"Get me a wrench," he orders, just like Pop-pop.

I run downstairs and fetch the toolbox. By the time I get back upstairs, the leak has slowed to a trickle.

"This stupid toilet," I say.

"Here, gimme that," Frankie says, and grabs a wrench and looks behind the toilet. "I think this is the thing that stops the water."

"You sure you know what you're doing?" I ask.

"Sure, sure," he says. "No problem."

He twists something and I hear a crack, and suddenly water starts spurting everywhere. A regular flood!

"Frankie!" I shout.

"It ain't my fault!" he shouts back.

My mind is whirling. I can't call my mother, because she's at work, and Me-me and Pop-pop are shopping.

"I'm calling Uncle Dominic," I say, and the minute the words leave my mouth, I know it's the right thing to do.

I call the store and Aunt Fulvia picks up.

"What's the matter, hon?" she asks.

"I gotta talk to Uncle Dominic," I say in a rush. "It's an emergency!"

Uncle Dominic gets on, and I explain to him what's happened. He pulls up and gets out of his car a few moments later, carrying a toolbox. With his slippers and his bloodstained apron from Falucci's Market, he's a sight to see.

"It won't stop," I say. "I don't know what to do."

Frankie's standing at the top of the stairs.

"You do this?" Uncle Dominic asks.

"What?" Frankie says. "It just broke. It's always breaking. Tell him!"

"He's right," I say.

When we reach the bathroom, Uncle Dominic takes one look behind the toilet and shakes his head. "Stay put. I gotta go down to the basement."

Frankie and me hold our breath, waiting, and suddenly the water stops.

"It stopped!" I yell.

Uncle Dominic comes back up a minute later.

"What'd you do?" Frankie asks him.

"I just shut off the water," he says.

"Jeez," Frankie says. "That was it? I could've done that!"

"Frankie," Uncle Dominic says, "I don't think plumbing's your calling."

Frankie waves his hand. "As if I'd wanna be a plumber."

Uncle Dominic gets down on his hands and knees by the toilet and does this and that. Then he goes back downstairs and turns the water back on. When he comes back up, he says, "That should do it."

"Is it okay to use?" I ask.

Uncle Dominic flushes experimentally. There's no flood!

"You're safe," he says.

Uncle Dominic and Frankie and me mop up all the water, and when we're finished, it looks good as new. Well, aside from the rugs being soaking wet and all the towels. We drag everything outside to hang on the clothesline.

"Come on, Frankie," Uncle Dominic says. "I'll give you a lift home."

"Thanks, Uncle Dominic," I say, and I mean it. "You saved my life."

"Anything for you, Princess," he says with a small smile.

As I lie in bed that night, I stare at my new red

coat hanging on the back of the door. It's beautiful, probably the most beautiful coat I've ever owned when it comes right down to it.

But when I hear the toilet flush above me, I know which uncle gave me the best present today.

CHAPTER SEVEN

The Translator

My mother's laughter wakes me up.

It's a light, happy laugh—a sound I'm not used to hearing.

I push back the covers and open the door to my room and go out to the parlor. I can see my mother through the screen door. She's standing on the porch talking to Mr. Mulligan. She's holding four bottles of milk.

"Pat," she says, and laughs again.

I open the screen door and they both stop talking.

"Hi, Bunny," she says. "You're up early."

"It's hot," I say. "Hi, Mr. Mulligan."

"Hello, Penny," he says with a big smile.

"Mr. Mulligan was just telling me how he might

be getting a new route. Isn't that interesting, Penny?" my mother asks.

"Real interesting," I say, trying not to roll my eyes.

"I better be off. Lots of deliveries yet," Mr. Mulligan says, and tips his hat. He walks back to his truck, whistling.

We go inside to the kitchen, and Mother pours a cup of coffee, smiling to herself. She didn't smile when I gave her the fox stole last night; she just shook her head and put it in the closet, saying, "Now, where would I ever wear this?"

"It's going to be just you and Me-me and Pop-pop for dinner tonight," she tells me. "I have to work late."

"Okay," I say. I feel bad for my mother sometimes. She works so hard. None of the other kids I know have mothers who have to work. But then, most of them have fathers.

"Do you have to work at your uncle's store today?" she asks.

"We have deliveries this afternoon."

Her mouth purses slightly. "Then be sure to give Me-me a hand with the chores this morning."

I go to my bedroom and come back a moment later.

"Here," I say, holding out a small envelope. "Uncle Ralphie paid me."

"Bunny," she says, "you don't have to give me your money."

"I want to," I say, going over to the Milk Money jar and dropping it in. "Maybe we can save up and buy a television."

"We'll see," she says, which means no.

"Are we going to Aunt Francine and Uncle Donald's for vacation this summer?" I ask.

"Yes," she says. "At the end of August."

"Do we have to?"

"But that house is right on the lake," my mother says, by which she means the house belongs to relatives and is free.

Aunt Francine is my mother's older sister. She and her husband have a cabin on Lake George in upstate New York, and we go there every summer. It should be fun, but it isn't, because I always have to watch their seven-year-old daughter, my cousin Lou Ellen. Lou Ellen's a brat.

Last summer she got mad because I wouldn't play dolls with her. That night when we were taking a bath together, she reached across and turned on the hot water faucet and it burned me on my back. Mother rushed me home to see Dr. Lathrop, our family doctor, because she didn't trust the doctor at the lake. I had to go to the hospital and everything. Dr. Lathrop had been in the army and knew all about burns and put this medicine on my back called Scarlet Red that stained everything I wore. I had to get a whole new wardrobe.

The worst part, though, was watching my mother. She went kind of crazy when I got burned. The entire drive home I kept telling her it didn't hurt. Dr. Lathrop said my nerve endings were destroyed, which is why I didn't feel any pain. I couldn't do anything for the rest of the summer: no playing, no baseball, no bicycle riding, no going to the beach, no nothing. I just lay on my stomach listening to the radio and Pop-pop burping. But Mother thought I was going to die. Even now I'm surprised she lets me leave the house.

"Well, I'm not taking any baths with Lou Ellen," I say.

"That's probably a good idea," she says, buttering a piece of toast and passing it to me. "Are you getting excited for your birthday? It's almost here."

"I guess," I say with a shrug. When I was little, I used to ask my mother for a father, but I haven't asked for that in a while.

"Twelve's a big birthday," she says.

Twelve has always seemed pretty old to me. The girls who are twelve are in seventh grade and worry about their hair and are always trying to borrow their older sisters' bras.

"What did you get when you were twelve?" I ask, curious.

"My first real piece of jewelry," she says.

"Really?"

"It was a single-strand pearl necklace. Me-me and Pop-pop said that twelve was old enough to take care of something precious. I still have it."

"I know that necklace," I say.

"I wore it to my very first dance. My dress was peach crepe de chine," she muses, looking out the window, twisting the ruby ring on her finger. It's her engagement ring from my father.

The sun is streaming through the green gauzy curtains, and my mother looks so beautiful standing there. She is the most beautiful woman I know when she smiles, which isn't nearly often enough.

"Did you kiss him?" I ask. "The boy you went to the dance with?"

"Penny!"

"Well, did you?"

"Now, what would you know about kissing, Bunny?"

Not much. I can't imagine kissing any boy,

certainly none of the ones I go to school with. How can you kiss a boy who you watched pick his nose in kindergarten?

My mother shakes herself and looks down at the watch on her wrist.

"Just look at the time! I'm going to be late for work at this rate," she says, and gives me a quick hug, her perfume swirling around me, lily of the valley.

Long after she's gone, I imagine my mother—young, beautiful, and wearing a peach crepe de chine dress—twirling under the moon in my father's arms as Bing Crosby croons "Dancing in the Dark."

Me-me's cleaning up the breakfast dishes when Pop-pop says, "Thought I'd take Penny for a stroll into town. Need me to pick up anything?"

Me-me smiles and says, "Let me get my list."

Across the table Pop-pop winks and I roll my eyes.

I'm just his excuse to go to the tobacco shop to buy cigars. He's not supposed to smoke cigars anymore because Me-me doesn't like the way they smell up the house, but he still buys them every chance he gets and smokes them secretly. There's a pile of cigar stubs behind the azalea bush in the backyard that's been growing for a while now.

Me-me hands me the list. She knows better than to give it to Pop-pop.

"Ready to tear up the pea patch, old girl?" Pop-pop asks me as he slaps on his hat.

"Ready," I say.

We start down the block. Pop-pop's walking pretty good with his cane. I've noticed lately that he doesn't have too much trouble walking when he wants to get cigars. It's only when Me-me wants him to take out the trash that his old war wound starts acting up.

"Hello, Mrs. Farro," Pop-pop calls.

Pop-pop was the block captain during World War II, so he knows everyone. During air-raid drills he had to go around the neighborhood making sure that people had their curtains drawn and their lights off; otherwise, the Germans and Japanese would know where to bomb us. Mrs. Dubrowski, who lives next door and is kind of eccentric, would never turn her lights off during the drills, no matter how many times Pop-pop tried to reason with her. Pop-pop said he thought that we were going to be bombed to kingdom come because of "that woman."

"Your tomatoes are looking well," he says.

"It's all this sun," Mrs. Farro says. "I think it's

our best harvest since the war."

Pop-pop says that during the war food was rationed, and near the end there wasn't much meat, so people started making burger patties using mashed baked beans and called them Truman-burgers after President Truman. Me-me says that there were butter shortages, so we used margarine. She said it came in white slabs, and to make it look better, you would knead in the yellow-orange coloring it came with. I still don't know what Germany and Japan had to do with us not having meat and butter. It's just one more thing I'll probably never understand, like why my mother doesn't like my father's family.

My father's family doesn't talk about the war, but Pop-pop sure does, every chance he gets. Pop-pop's favorite story is about a friend of his who was a translator. This fella was in college, at Harvard, and the government drafted him and taught him Japanese, and it was his job to interrogate the Japanese prisoners of war in California. The information he got from the prisoners helped the government decide to drop the atomic bomb on Nagasaki. The first atomic bomb was dropped on Hiroshima, but after the second bomb was dropped on Nagasaki, the Japanese gave up.

Pop-pop showed me a photograph of the translator at the surrender of the Japanese at Tokyo Bay. He looks sort of sad. You'd think he'd be happy the war was over, but I guess he wasn't.

Sometimes I feel like a translator. Mother is always asking me this or that about my father's family, and I have to try to figure out what she means, like it's a different language. Certain things just get her upset. Like when she finds out that the uncles have taken me to Shady Grove Cemetery. I don't know why this bothers her so much; you'd think she'd be happy I visit my father, but it has the opposite effect. Or if I go to the Catholic church with Nonny, she gets angry even though she doesn't go to church herself. Or if they give me a fancy present or something like that. There are times when I just wish I knew the language she was speaking.

"Can we get lunch at the Sweete Shoppe?" I ask Pop-pop. The Sweete Shoppe is a luncheonette that has a full fountain. They make awfully good egg creams and ice cream sundaes.

"Got to eat, I suppose," he says, and then mutters, "Reckon any place is safer than your grandmother's kitchen."

The Sweete Shoppe is nearly empty; it's too

early for the lunch rush. There's a lady with her daughter sitting in a booth and a man sitting at the counter sipping coffee.

We take seats at the counter, and the waitress comes over to take our order. "What can I get for you?"

"Hamburger deluxe," Pop-pop says, and turns to me. "What'll you have?"

"A sundae with butter pecan ice cream, please."

Pop-pop looks at me. "That's your whole lunch?"

"Uh-huh," I say.

"Don't tell your grandmother," he says.

The food arrives and I take a bite of my sundae. It's delicious. The hot fudge tastes perfect with the butter pecan ice cream.

I watch Pop-pop as he carefully takes the lettuce and tomato and pickle and onion off the hamburger and sets them on a little plate on the side. He does the same with the fries.

"Why don't you just order a plain hamburger?" I ask.

"I like the deluxe," he says. "I like knowing I can eat it if I want to."

"But you never do," I say.

"What is this? An interrogation?"

Pop-pop polishes off his hamburger in about

four bites and then leans back and burps loudly. I pretend that I don't know him.

We pay and go back out and start down the street again. A bunch of men in army uniforms walk by us and enter the VFW hall. Usually on the Fourth of July, all the veterans get dressed up and have a parade. Pop-pop says that after the war ended, there was a big ticker-tape parade in New York City. Now *that's* a parade I'd like to have seen.

Pop-pop stops outside the tobacco shop. "I'll just be a minute."

I sit down on the bench, where another kid is already sitting. His name is Robert and he's skinny and only in second grade and he's always sitting out here.

"Want one?" he asks, showing me a handful of gum balls from his pocket.

"Thanks," I say, and take a red one. It's warm and melting, but I pop it in my mouth anyway.

"Where's Frankie?" he asks.

"At home, I think," I say. I'm not surprised he knows Frankie. Everyone does. It's just the kind of boy Frankie is.

"What's your father smoke?" I ask.

"Camels," he says. "What about yours?"

"Cigars," I say. "It's my grandfather."

He nods wisely. "I thought he looked kind of old."

A boy named Arthur comes up with his father.

"Wait here with the other kids, you hear?" his father tells him.

Arthur sits down next to Robert. We're like the three monkeys: See No Evil, Hear No Evil, Speak No Evil.

Next to the tobacco shop is a café. There are always old Italian men there, drinking dark coffee that looks like tar served in little cups and reading the Italian-language newspapers. They're newspapers that are printed in Italian so people can find out what's going on if they don't know English. Uncle Nunzio told me that my father used to write for one of these Italian-language newspapers every once in a while, although his main job was writing for a regular English-language newspaper.

"*Buongiorno, signorina,*" they call to me.

"*Buongiorno,*" I call back.

"How's the professor's little girl today?" one of them asks.

"Good, thanks," I say.

They all loved my father. He used to help them when he was alive, translating and writing letters, because most of them didn't know English. A lot of them fought for Italy in World War I.

I've always thought it was confusing that Italy was on our side in World War I and on the other side in World War II. It must have been hard for my uncles who fought, because they might have been fighting against their own family. Maybe that's why they don't like to talk about the war.

Stanley Teitelzweig and his older brother, Jack, walk by.

"Hi, Penny," Jack says, stopping in front of me.

"Hi," I say back, feeling a butterfly tickle in my stomach.

"Having a good summer?" Jack asks.

"Sure," I say shyly. I've never really been interested in boys before, unlike some of the other girls at school, but Jack's different. Something about his curly dark hair and his green eyes. He sure is cute!

Stanley's staring at my head.

"Say, Penny, what happened to your hair?"

"Uh—uh—uh," I stammer, "I got it cut."

"Boy, you should go to a different place next time," Stanley says.

I close my eyes. When I open them, Pop-pop is standing next to Jack.

"These boys bothering you, Penny?" Pop-pop asks with a scowl.

"Pop-pop," I say quickly.

"They look like trouble to me," he says, and burps loudly.

"Come on," Stanley says, grabbing Jack by his arm. "We're going to be late."

As they walk away, Jack looks back at me. I can see the shocked expression on his face from where I'm sitting.

"I got rid of them pretty good, didn't I?" Pop-pop says in a pleased voice.

"You sure did," I say, and sigh.

CHAPTER EIGHT

Nonny's Underwear

It's a hot July day, but it's nice and cool in Nonny's basement.

Frankie and me are helping with the laundry. I feed the wet clothes through the wringer like Me-me taught me. The clothes get squeezed through the rollers, and the water is wrung out of them. Me-me always says to be careful, because you can get your fingers pulled in the wringer if you're not paying close attention.

Nonny's upstairs, arguing with Aunt Gina.

"Mother Falucci," Aunt Gina says, her voice loud, "I counted three eggs this morning. I would appreciate it if you'd at least ask me before taking things from my refrigerator."

Nonny shouts back in Italian, and Aunt Gina

yells, "You know very well how to speak English!"

"I don't know how Uncle Paulie stands it. They're always at each other," Frankie says, shaking his head.

Above us, a dish goes flying, and a pair of Aunt Gina–like heels clip-clops out the front door.

"Sounds like Nonny won," Frankie says with a small smile.

I love Nonny. She's a tough old lady.

"Remember the kite?" I ask.

Frankie smirks. "Bobby's lucky he still has both hands."

One time when we were little, we were playing outside in front of Nonny's with a brand-new kite that the uncles gave us. This older neighborhood bully named Bobby Rocco came along and tried to take the kite from Frankie. But Frankie, being Frankie, wouldn't let that kite go, even though Bobby Rocco was twice as big as him. They started tussling, and Bobby just smacked Frankie like he was a fly, and poor Frankie fell on the ground.

Well, Nonny was watching from the front window, and when she saw this, she grabbed up a meat cleaver and came running out, waving it at Bobby. She said that if he ever smacked Frankie again, he wouldn't have anything to smack with—she'd chop

off both his hands herself. He hasn't bothered
Frankie since.

"So what do you think you're getting for your
birthday?" Frankie asks.

Every year the uncles get me a big gift. Last
year we went to the circus and then for a lobster
dinner afterward. The year before that I got a
fancy dollhouse. Frankie gets presents from the
uncles on his birthday, too, but not as big as mine.
The uncles are always trying to make up for my
father being dead.

"I don't know," I say, although I've been dropping hints about a new bicycle to replace the one
Pop-pop ran over.

"Do you think Uncle Dom would teach me how
to drive?" Frankie asks. "I figure of all the uncles,
I have the best chance with him." What he means
is Uncle Dominic is strange and does things
nobody else does, like live in his car when there's
a perfectly good bedroom in the house.

"Why do you want to drive?"

"So I can get a real job—you know, make good
money," he says.

"Frankie," I say, "you're too young."

"Hey, Miss Smarty-Pants, I can drive if I want.
Joey Fantone is driving already and he's fourteen,"
Frankie says.

Joey Fantone is almost six feet tall. The coach from the basketball team started talking to him when he was in elementary school.

"But he looks like he's eighteen," I say. "And he's not supposed to be driving."

"You're saying I don't look old enough to drive?"

"Yeah. That's what I'm saying." I look at him more closely. "What's this all about, anyhow?"

Frankie looks down. "Pop lost his job again."

Uncle Angelo is always losing his job. It probably doesn't help that he likes to drink whiskey a lot. The other uncles used to give him money and help him out with work, get him jobs and everything, but then there was a big fight and now Uncle Angelo says he doesn't want "nobody's handouts." But I know that Nonny and all the aunts sneak Aunt Teresa money, and Aunt Fulvia lets her get anything she wants from the store for free.

"When we came home yesterday afternoon, he was on the couch. He said they just fired him for no reason. No reason at all."

"Oh, Frankie," I say, and as soon as the words leave my mouth, Frankie's face darkens. If there's one thing Frankie can't stand, it's pity.

We work in silence for a little while, and then I

say, "Maybe you should ask Uncle Dominic. You never know."

"You're just saying that," he says.

"Yeah, I am," I say, and laugh, and he cracks a smile and I know we're okay again.

Frankie holds up a slinky-looking red satin slip. "Must be Aunt Gina's," he says.

"Sure isn't Nonny's," I say.

"Hey, you think Nonny has black underwear?" Frankie asks.

"I don't know," I say, and shrug. "Maybe. Everything else is black."

"Ain't you curious?"

"Not really."

"Come on. She wears black all the time, even in the summer," Frankie says.

"It's a tradition, you know. Mourning clothes. Because of my father. Grandpa, too, I guess."

"Have I got an idea!" he says, a note of excitement in his voice. "We case her room."

"Why don't you just ask her?" I say.

"Nah, let's spy on her," he says.

"Frankie . . ."

"Well?" he demands, a bulldog expression on his face. "You gonna help or what?"

Maybe because I want to know too, or maybe

because Frankie is my best friend, my cousin, and I'd do just about anything to make him stop thinking about how his father will never be any good, I say what he wants to hear.

I say, "Sure."

Nonny gives us lunch in the dining room. It's ricotta-ball soup, which is really good. Nonny looks pleased when Frankie and me ask for seconds. There's nothing she likes better than feeding people.

The telephone rings. Since Aunt Gina's out, Nonny picks it up and listens for a minute and then says, "Nobody home. Good-bye."

Frankie shakes his head. Nonny always does this if the person on the other end doesn't speak Italian. She's scared to talk on the phone.

After lunch Nonny goes upstairs. She takes her bath in the afternoon, and then a nap, and Frankie figures that this is the perfect time to look in her room. We pretend to play cards, but when we hear the water start running, Frankie nods to me.

"Go," he whispers.

"I'm going, I'm going," I say.

I creep upstairs, pausing outside the bathroom to make sure that Nonny's in there. I can hear her humming, a soft song that sounds sort of familiar, like something you would sing to a baby. I hurry down the hall to her bedroom. I feel like I'm breaking the law by going in there; it's just not something you do.

The room is filled with large pieces of heavy, dark furniture, and there's a crucifix hanging over the bed. In the corner is a washstand with a pitcher that I know she brought over from Italy, the only thing that survived the trip. The pitcher has been cracked and glued back together, and I can't help but think it reminds me of Nonny: small but tough enough to leave a whole world behind.

There's a big four-drawer dresser, and I open the top drawer, the drawer where most people keep their socks. And sure enough, there are rolled-up balls of black stockings and neat stacks of black lace handkerchiefs. The next drawer down has black sweaters and blouses, but no underwear. The next one down has men's clothes, tidy piles of trousers and button-up shirts with carefully mended collars. With a start, I realize that they must have belonged to my grandfather. I don't know very much about Grandpa, except that he played the mandolin. He died before I was born. Frankie says he heard Grandpa had some sort of fit and just keeled over. I wonder how long Nonny's had his clothes in here, and then I wonder how come it's always Frankie who's coming up with these schemes and always me who's doing them.

Finally, I open the bottom drawer, and lying right on top is something that's black and silky and I think I've hit pay dirt. Only it's just a silk kerchief, not underwear, but when I move it, I find something else.

It's a photograph of Nonny holding a fat, round pudgy baby dressed in a white gown on her lap. I turn over the photograph and see that someone's written "Alfredo." It's my father! They must have still been in Italy; they didn't come over until my father was two. All the other kids were born here.

Nonny is young in the photograph—her hair hasn't turned white yet, and her skin is smooth, like porcelain. The photographer has caught the exact moment when she's looking down at the baby and not at the camera, and the expression on her face is one of such happiness, such joy, that I just stare at it. She looks like the happiest mother in the whole world.

Underneath the photograph is a black photo album, and I open it. It's filled with newspaper clippings—articles written by my father. It looks like Nonny kept everything he ever wrote. Most of the articles are in English, but a few are in Italian.

I start reading the articles, and it's like he's in the room with me, I can hear his voice so clearly in my head.

This looks to be a close election with—

The bathroom door opens and closes, and there's the soft pad of footsteps making their way down the hall. I put the album back and shut the drawer just in time. Nonny opens the door wearing her bathrobe, which is black, naturally.

"Penny?" she says, surprised.

"Uh, hi, Nonny," I say.

I'm expecting her to yell at me for being in her room, but instead she just closes the door and walks over to her dressing table. She sits down on the little stool and undoes the single tortoiseshell comb and then hands me her brush. I used to brush her hair when I was a little girl.

The brush is heavy, with a thick wooden handle that fits my hand and bristles that are bare in places. I carefully brush out her hair. It's long, almost all the way down her back. After her hair is smooth and free of tangles, I twist it into one thick braid, tying it at the end with a piece of black ribbon she hands me.

"There," I say. "You look real good, Nonny."

Nonny takes off her bathrobe and there it is: a long white slip, an old-fashioned cotton one with handmade lace at the hem. I look in her eyes, and I suddenly know why she wears black. It's her shield, her armor in a country where she can't speak the language, where she's still afraid after all these years to talk on the phone or answer the door because she might not understand what someone's saying. It's her way of looking fierce, of hiding the fact that she's old and tired and homesick.

"*Tesoro mio,*" she says, her voice weary.

I help her into bed and tuck the sheet high around her neck. She is asleep before I even leave the room.

Frankie's waiting for me when I come downstairs.

"Well?" he asks.

"You were right," I lie. "Black."

He slaps his palm on his leg. "I knew it!"

But I know that it doesn't really matter. Black, white, or purple underwear, she's still my Nonny.

CHAPTER NINE

The Slider

Uncle Dominic says the thing about a slider is that you never see it coming. It's the one pitch that can fool even the best batter.

When I get home from delivering orders with Frankie, I find Mother in her bedroom, sitting at her dressing table. She's wearing a dress I haven't see before. It's lemon yellow and strapless. It looks glamorous and shows off her freckled shoulders.

"Are we going out for dinner?" I ask. We don't go to restaurants very often and, believe me, it's a real treat when we do.

"Actually," she says, "I'm going out. Me-me's made hamburger-olive loaf for you."

I groan. Me-me's hamburger-olive loaf is so bad, it should be in jail.

"You going out with Connie again?" I ask.

She turns around on her little stool and looks me in the eye. "Mr. Mulligan asked me out to dinner and dancing."

"Mr. Mulligan?" I say.

"Yes."

"The milkman?"

"Yes."

"You're going out to dinner with the milkman?" I blurt out.

My mother's voice doesn't have to get loud to show her disapproval. "His name is Mr. Mulligan, Penny, and he's a very nice man. And there's nothing wrong with being a milkman. He does quite well for himself."

"Hold it," I say, remembering the two of them talking on the porch. "Is this the first time you've gone out with him?"

She hesitates and then says, "No."

"You've been dating him? For how long?"

She looks out the window, idly picking the dead leaves off the plant on the windowsill. "A little while."

This is even worse than Me-me's hamburger-olive loaf!

I look at her ring finger and notice that it's bare; the engagement ring is gone!

"Mother, where's your ring?"

"Penny," she says, her voice cool, "I need to fin-ish getting ready. We'll talk in the morning."

"But—"

She cuts me off with a look.

"Mr. Mulligan will be here at six," she says, and then she turns her back to me and starts putting on her lipstick.

I stay awake waiting for my mother to come home. Scarlett O'Hara keeps me company in the parlor.

All these years I've wanted a father and this is what I get? The milkman? What does she see in him? My real father was handsome as a movie star, not going bald like Mr. Mulligan.

"I can't believe she's dating the milkman, Scarlett O'Hara," I tell my dog.

She whines like she's as shocked as me.

Pop-pop wanders through and says, "What're you doing up?"

"I can't sleep," I say.

"What?" he asks. "What?"

"I said, 'I can't sleep,'" I say loudly.

"Drink some warm milk."

"I hate milk," I mutter. "Especially now."

"Hmph," he says.

When I finally hear the car pull up, it's late, nearly midnight. I creep over to the front window and peek out.

Mr. Mulligan is walking around to the passenger side of the car. He opens the door for my mother and helps her out. He whispers something in her ear and she laughs. Then he leans over and . . .

Kisses her! Right on the lips!

At that exact moment, Scarlett O'Hara tinkles on the carpet.

My sentiments exactly.

A few days later, on Saturday, I go into the kitchen and open the refrigerator and there's a big plate of delicious-looking fried chicken just sitting there. It's almost lunchtime and I'm hungry, so I take a leg and am about to bite into it when I hear my mother say:

"That's for later, Penny."

"For what?" I ask.

"I know you're a bit upset about Mr. Mulligan, but he's very nice," my mother says quickly. "Why, when I told him how much of a Dodgers fan you are, he offered to come over and listen to the ball game with you."

"What?"

"So you can get to know him," she says. "Isn't that wonderful?"

Wonderful? Is she *pazza*?

"But I'm supposed to listen to the game with Uncle Dominic," I lie.

"Just this once you can listen to it here," she says.

"I can't. I promised him," I say.

She frowns. "You were over there yesterday and practically every day this week."

"So what? I like it there. They have fun. They laugh. They eat food that tastes good. Their toilet's not always leaking!"

"Penny," she says.

But it doesn't matter. Some line has been crossed and there's no crossing back.

"They talk about my father!" I shout. "They talk about him all the time. Not like here. It's like you're embarrassed of him or something. Why won't you talk about him? Why?"

She stares at me and I think she's going to say something, but then it's like a shutter closes over her eyes, and she shakes her head.

"Because there's nothing to say," she says.

We sit in the parlor listening to the game. I don't know what's worse: having to wear a babyish ruffled pink skirt or listening to Mr. Mulligan.

The whole game, Mr. Mulligan's been trying to make conversation with me, asking me about my summer. There's nothing worse than someone talking during a ball game. I've been doing my best to ignore him, but it's already the eighth inning, and I swear I've only heard about two minutes.

"And there's the pitch," the announcer says over the radio.

"Say, Penny," Mr. Mulligan says, a cheery little smile on his face, "you looking forward to starting seventh grade?"

"Shh," I say.

"Pardon me?" he asks.

"Can you be quiet? I can't hear the game," I say.

"Penny," my mother says. "Apologize immediately, young lady."

"Why?" I ask. "He's been talking the whole time!"

My mother shoots me a look.

"Ellie, it's fine. I'm sure this is all a surprise to her," Mr. Mulligan says in a soothing voice, reaching over and clasping her hand gently.

"Ellie?" I say. "You let him call you Ellie?"

"Penny," my mother says, "there's no call to be so dramatic."

I look at Mr. Mulligan's beefy hand on my mother's slender one, and I see my whole life changing in the blink of an eye. No more uncles, no more Pop-pop and Me-me. It'll be boring old Mr. Mulligan talking through the ball game. I can't believe I ever thought he was funny.

The next thing I know I'm leaping up from my chair and racing out the front door, Mother calling my name. I'm running down the street, my legs pumping fast, my skirt flying in the air. All I can think is Mr. Mulligan is going to end up being my father, and I can't bear it. Everything'll change; my whole life will be ruined.

I run and run, like I've just hit a ball to left field and am rounding the bases. Mrs. Farro's is first, and the Sweete Shoppe is second, and Falucci's Market is third, and then I'm rounding third, heading for home, and I can see Uncle Dominic's car—he's in the front seat, the window down, the portable radio on. I don't even ask him; I just fling open the passenger door and throw myself in and the tears start pouring down my cheeks, pouring and pouring like they're never gonna stop. I'm bawling my head off, crying so hard, you'd think the fire department would hire me.

"Princess," Uncle Dominic says, alarm in his voice. "What's wrong?"

But I can't speak; I'm too busy crying, and it must scare Uncle Dominic, because he grabs me by the shoulders and gives me a little shake.

"What happened? Did some boy touch you?" he demands, his voice urgent.

That snaps me out of it like a blast of cold water.

"No," I say. "Nothing like that."

"Oh," he says, and his shoulders relax immediately. "Okay, then. What's with the waterworks?"

"It's Mother," I say.

"Something happened to your mother?"

"She's dating the milkman!"

He blinks.

"He came over to the house and talked through the whole game," I say.

"The milkman," Uncle Dominic says.

"Yes! The milkman!" And then I burst into tears again.

He digs out his handkerchief. "Here. Come on now, it's not so bad."

This from a man who lives in a car and talks to dogs?

"Don't you understand? What if they get married? What if he becomes my father?"

"Then you have a new father," he says. "Right?"

"But he's all wrong! He's not the kind of father I want!"

"Why? Does he drink?"

"I don't think so," I say. "Unless you count milk."

"That's good," he says. "Does he have a job?"

"He's a milkman," I say.

"Sober and employed," Uncle Dominic says. "What more could you ask for?"

"It's just that I want someone like, like . . ." and my throat closes up.

"Your father?" he finishes.

"Maybe you can marry Mother?" I ask, and start talking fast. "You know all about me. And you know how to fix the toilet. Even Me-me will like that."

Uncle Dominic just shakes his head sadly. "Princess, your mother and me, we just ain't never gonna be like that."

I lean back against the seat. "It's not fair."

"Life's not fair," Uncle Dominic says, and I know he's right. After all, he could be playing for the Dodgers right now instead of listening to them on the radio.

"Are you sure you won't think about it?"

He shakes his head.

"Why did she have to pick the milkman?" I mutter.

"Look at it this way," he says, putting his arm around my shoulder. "At least you'll get a lot of free milk."

Uncle Dominic drives me home. My mother's sitting on the front porch swing when we get there, and Mr. Mulligan's car is gone.

"Think she's mad?" I ask Uncle Dominic.

"Knowing your mother, I'd say so," he says.

"But she threw me a slider, Uncle Dominic! Honest, I never saw it coming."

He shrugs. "That's the game, Princess."

"Well, I struck out," I grumble, and I open the car door and get out. I poke my head back through the window. "What should I do?"

"Apologize and then stay out of her way. She'll cool off."

"Thanks," I say.

"Anytime, Princess," he says.

I wait until he's driven away to walk up the steps.

"I'm sorry," I say to her.

My mother doesn't have to say a word. The door banging behind her as she goes into the house says it all.

CHAPTER TEN

The Water Boy's Treasure

Frankie thinks it's hilarious.

"Your mother's dating Milky Mulligan?" He guffaws.

We're sweeping up the store. It's me and Frankie's job to put down new sawdust—otherwise the blood from the back gets tracked everywhere.

"Does he smell like old cheese?" Frankie asks. "You know, how milk bottles sometimes get that old-cheese smell when they're left out in the sun?"

"Frankie," I say.

"Boy, if they get married, you'll be Penny Milky Mulligan."

"Shut up."

He bursts out laughing. "You can serve milk instead of champagne at the wedding! No, wait, I got it! *Milk shakes!*"

"Knock it off!" I say, and wave my broom at him threateningly.

"Hey!" he protests. "I was just fooling."

"It's not funny."

He snickers. "You think maybe you can get me a deal on cottage cheese?"

The bell on the door rings and Uncle Sally walks in, which is a good thing because I am a step away from whacking Frankie right in the kisser. Not that it would do any good.

"Hey, kids," Uncle Sally says, and ruffles Frankie's hair, even though he's barely an inch taller than Frankie.

"How's your mother, Penny?" Uncle Sally asks.

I want to say, She's wrecking my life, but instead I say, "She's good, thanks."

"A great lady, your mother," he says wistfully.

Uncle Sally has a crush on my mother, and he's always asking after her. I don't have the heart to tell him he's not her type. Not that I can see her dating Mr. Mulligan, either, but at least he comes up to her chin.

"You got in any of that tongue I like?" Uncle Sally asks Uncle Ralphie.

"In the locker. Dominic's been saving some for you," Uncle Ralphie says, leading him into the back room.

I turn to Frankie and make a gagging sound. I don't know how you can eat a tongue, even if it is from a cow.

"What is it with him and the tongue?" I ask.

Frankie shrugs and says, "Maybe it's 'cause he's such a big talker."

Uncle Sally always knows what's going on in town. If someone sneezes, he knows about it.

Outside, a Sister of Mercy, one of the teachers at Frankie's school, walks past the window. The sister looks in and catches sight of Frankie and narrows her eyes.

Frankie shakes his head and says, "Those Sisters of Mercy. They ain't got no mercy."

We load up the old sawdust into buckets and carry them around back to the garbage cans. Uncle Sally and Uncle Ralphie's voices drift through the back door of the office, which is propped open.

"So I was talking to old man Garboella," Uncle Sally is saying, "and boy did he ever tell me some story."

I motion Frankie over to the door.

"Get this," Uncle Sally says. "He told me that the Water boy once told him that he had a bunch of money hidden somewhere at the house."

"The Water boy" was my late grandfather Falucci. He got his nickname because of his first job on a construction site when he came to America. It just sort of stuck.

"He said he buried it in the ground," Uncle Sally says.

Frankie's eyes widen.

Inside, Uncle Ralphie chuckles. "Yeah? He tell you where?"

"If I knew, I'd be over there with a shovel right now," Uncle Sally says, and they both laugh.

This doesn't surprise me all that much. Nonny does something similar. She pins dollar bills in the hems of drapes, squirrels them away under chair cushions. I once found five dollars under one of the Queenies' beds, all matted with dog hair. I don't know why they don't put money in banks like everyone else, but they just don't.

Frankie grabs my hand and squeezes. I already know what he's thinking. He's got the shovels lined up and is figuring out where to start digging.

"Do you believe it?" he whispers, his face flushed with excitement.

"I don't know. Maybe."

"Think of all that dough! Then we don't never gotta worry again."

By which he means that he doesn't ever have to worry about his father losing his job again.

I wrinkle my nose. "But if it is true, how're we

gonna find it? We can't go digging up the yard."

Frankie's face turns sly.

"Says who?"

"So you need any yard work done, Uncle Paulie?" Frankie is asking.

We're over at Nonny's, sitting in the upstairs kitchen. Frankie thinks that the easiest way to find the treasure is to just work in the yard. We'll figure out where the treasure is buried and then come back at night and dig it up.

Uncle Paulie raises his eyebrows. "You volunteering?"

"You bet," Frankie says.

Uncle Paulie leans back and sips his coffee. "I guess the bushes could use a prune."

"Sure," Frankie says eagerly.

"And there are a few sticks that need picking up."

"Sticks, you got it," Frankie says.

"And while you're at it, you can cut the grass."

Frankie's smile droops a little, but he says, "Be glad to."

"Thanks, kid," Uncle Paulie says, and turns back to his paper.

Two hours later we're still picking up sticks in the front yard. They're all over the place. A big tree is dying and has been dropping them every-where. We haven't even gotten to the backyard yet.

"I'm beat," I say to Frankie.

"Quit complaining," he says.

"But we're never going to find anything at this rate."

"Grandpa must have left some sort of marker or something," Frankie says.

"How come?"

"Because otherwise how would *he* find it?"

I guess he does have a point. Still, I think it's like looking for a needle in a haystack, but I don't say anything.

"I'm gonna get something to drink," I say.

As I walk away, I hear Frankie grumble to him-self. "A few sticks. Right. And I'll sell you a bridge to China while I'm at it."

I go into the house. It's quiet except for the sound of music floating downstairs. Uncle Paulie's gone to work and Nonny's visiting her old-lady friends. I help myself to a ginger ale and then wan-der out into the hallway.

"Hello," I call.

"Who's that?" Aunt Gina calls back.

"It's me, Penny," I say.

"Come on up, doll," she says.

I like Aunt Gina. She's the most interesting

aunt, in my opinion. She's not afraid to say what she thinks. Also, she's the only one of the aunts who doesn't have any kids, but nobody ever talks about that.

Aunt Gina is in her bedroom. It's a real fancy bedroom, done all in pink. There are pink chenille bedspreads on her and Uncle Paulie's twin beds, and her makeup table has a flouncy matching pink skirt. Her dresser is covered with fancy bottles of perfume and all sorts of jars of makeup and lipsticks, and the whole room smells like Evening in Paris. She's got a record player in the corner, and it's playing Nat King Cole. I love this room. It's what I imagine a movie star's bedroom looks like.

Aunt Gina's standing in her slip studying two dresses lying on one of the beds.

"Which one, you think?" she asks me.

"For what?" I say.

She squints and takes a puff on her cigarette. "Atlantic City. We're going there Friday night for our anniversary. Dinner and dancing. The works."

I study the dresses. One's emerald-green silk with a straight skirt and the other one is red satin with a full skirt.

"The red one," I say. "That's a dancing dress."

She nods approvingly. "You got a good eye, doll."

"Try it on," I say.

I sit back on the bed and watch Aunt Gina shimmy into the dress. The material clings to her curvy figure and she looks beautiful. She slips on high heels and gives a few good twirls. The skirt flies up, showing off strong, slim legs. Aunt Gina used to be a dancer with the Rockettes before she married Uncle Paulie. She danced at Radio City Music Hall and met lots of famous entertainers.

"Come here," she says, motioning me over to her dressing table. "On the stool."

I sit on the pink stool with the ruffle, feeling like Cinderella meeting her fairy godmother.

Aunt Gina shakes her head at the state of my hair.

"I know, I know," I say.

She picks up a thick brush and does this and that and takes a few pins and clips my hair behind my ears and flips it so that it falls all soft and pretty around my face. "That's better," she says. "You tell that grandmother of yours to stop giving you those home perms."

"You try telling her," I say.

She laughs and pats my curls. "You're real pretty, you know that? I'm surprised the boys aren't after you already."

They won't ever be after me if Pop-pop keeps chasing them off, I think.

"You spend too much time with that no-good cousin of yours," she says.

"Frankie? He's good," I say.

"You watch him," she says. "I've known boys like him. He's headed for trouble with a capital *T*."

I look at her in the mirror and imagine her kicking her away across the stage at Radio City Music Hall.

"You ever miss dancing?" I ask.

"Every day," she says. "But that's life, right, doll?"

"Why'd you quit?"

She gives a little laugh. "Your Uncle Paulie liked dating a dancer; he just didn't like the idea of having a wife who was one. Your grandmother wasn't much help, either."

"Nonny wanted you to quit dancing?"

"You got that right," she says, pursing her lips to apply bright-red lipstick. "And let me tell you, what your grandmother Falucci wants, she gets." She pauses, her reflection looking back at me from the mirror. "You know, your father was the only one who didn't give me a hard time about dancing."

"Really?"

"Yeah," she says. "Freddy was a good egg."

"I wish I could've seen you dance," I say.

She smiles and whirls around. "You can, doll. Turn up that record player."

As Frankie picks up sticks in the yard, I sit on the bed and watch Aunt Gina give the best show any Rockette has ever given.

It's so good, I swear I can hear the applause.

Frankie gets all excited when I tell him about Aunt Gina and Uncle Paulie going to Atlantic City.

"Now here it is," Frankie says. "We sneak over after they leave and start digging. I think I know where it might be. There's this spot where there's a smooth stone, kind of near the bushes, like a marker, you know? It's gotta be the place!"

"I don't know, Frankie," I say.

"Come on," he says. "Just think of all that dough."

In the end I give in. It's Frankie, after all.

The night of the dig, I try to act normal. I take a bath and put on my pajamas and give Mother a hard time about wanting to stay up late until finally she sends me to bed. I wait until the house is dark and quiet, and then I slip on my clothes and sneak out the back door. It's handy having my bedroom on the first floor.

Frankie's waiting for me on his bicycle behind a tree.

"Ready, palsy-walsy?" he asks.

I wrap my arms around his waist, and we pedal off down the street.

Nonny's house is dark and quiet when we get there. Friday is Uncle Dominic's poker night, so we don't have to worry about him.

"You think she's asleep?" Frankie asks.

"House looks dark," I say.

He leads me over to a row of bushes and points to a small smooth stone on the ground. "See, don't that look like a marker to you?"

"Maybe."

"Here," he says, handing me one of the shovels he stowed earlier today. He picks up the other one, and we start digging.

"If Mother finds out I'm not home, I'm gonna get it," I mutter.

"Quit worrying," he says. "We're gonna be famous. I can see the headline now: 'Boy Detective Finds Hidden Treasure'!"

"What about me?" I ask.

He thinks for a moment. "Maybe it could say: 'Boy Detective and Trusty Assistant Find Hidden Treasure.'"

"Gee, thanks."

"Say, what are you gonna do with your share of the loot?" he asks.

"Buy tickets to a Dodgers game." I've never been to one. Mother says ball games aren't appropriate for young girls. I want to tell her it's not appropriate to date milkmen who talk over the play-by-play.

My shovel hits something hard. "I think I found it!" I whisper.

"Move, move," Frankie commands. Using his bare hands, he digs like mad and pulls an old metal box out of the ground.

We share an excited look. He opens the lid, but instead of stacks of bills, there's a pile of dirt and what looks like bones and a small skull.

"Is that a bone?" I ask.

"What?" Frankie says. "Where's the money?"

There's a small disk of metal with writing on it. "It's Queenie I," I say. "Or maybe it's Queenie II. I can't tell. It's too dark."

Frankie snorts in disgust. "You kidding me?"

All of a sudden I hear barking. The Queenies are going crazy, yipping up a storm.

"Those dumb dogs," Frankie whispers.

"Maybe they're not so dumb," I whisper back. "Maybe they know we're out here digging up their friends."

Then I hear shouting from the back door.

"I call the *polizia*!" Nonny shouts.

"It's Nonny!" I whisper.

Nonny's standing there in her black bathrobe, waving something. It's dark, so she can't see who we are.

"Oh, brother," Frankie says. "Where'd she get a gun?"

"Gun? What gun?"

Before Frankie can say anything, there's a loud blast and he shoves me hard and says, "Run!"

We take off into the bushes, running through Uncle Nunzio's backyard, and then the next one, our hearts pounding in our chests. We run and run and run and don't stop until we're far away.

"My bike!" Frankie gasps. "It's still at the house!"

"I'm not going back," I say, trying to catch my breath.

"A lot of good you are," he gripes, and starts walking back toward Nonny's.

"You know what the headline's gonna be tomorrow morning if Nonny catches you?" I call.

"What?"

"'Dumb Boy Shot by Own Grandmother.'"

CHAPTER ELEVEN

More Peas, Please

The next morning is Saturday, and when I go into the kitchen, my mother is there.

She's wearing an apron and humming as she slices an onion on the big wooden cutting board. There's a raw chicken on the table and a pot of something bubbling on the stove. Mother only cooks when we have company. She's scared that Me-me's cooking will poison the guests.

"What's all this?" I ask.

Her hand pauses in midair over the chopping board. "We're having a guest for dinner tonight."

"Who?" I ask.

"Mr. Mulligan," she says.

"What?"

"Penny," she says, and there's a warning note in her voice.

At that moment Pop-pop walks in and sits down at the table with a heavy thud. He looks at the dinner preparation in surprise.

"Pope coming for dinner?" he asks.

"Not likely," I mutter.

"I got a new one for you. What do you call a hundred thousand Frenchmen with their hands in the air?" Pop-pop asks me.

I just look at him.

"The French army!" he says, and guffaws.

"That's not very funny," I say.

"Not funny?" he scowls. "Ain't ya got a sense of humor?"

My mother slams down the knife and visibly composes herself.

"Daddy," she says loudly, "you are going to behave yourself tonight, aren't you?"

"What are you talking about?" he says. "What's tonight?"

"Pat's coming for dinner, remember? I told you yesterday."

"Pat? Pat who?"

"Pat Mulligan!" she says in exasperation.

He stares at her a moment and then rubs his chin thoughtfully. "No need to shout. I can hear you fine. I ain't deaf."

The doorbell rings. I jump up.

My mother looks at me. "Where are you going?"

"To play ball with Frankie," I say. "That's him."

"Be back early. Mr. Mulligan's coming at five-thirty, so I want you clean and dressed by the time he gets here. That means a bath," she says, like I'm six. "I'll lay a dress out for you."

"You wanna brush my teeth, too?" I ask.

"No smart talk from you, young lady," she says. "Or you won't be going anywhere."

"Wait a minute," Pop-pop says. "Does this mean I have to wear a necktie?"

Frankie's waiting on the porch with his baseball mitts, grinning from ear to ear.

"You were right!" he says. "We made the paper!"

"What?"

"Look! The police blotter!" he says, and pulls a scrap of newsprint out of his back pocket.

Suspected Intruder Reported

I look around quickly. "Shh! Don't show that to anybody!"

"What's the matter with you?" he says. "We're famous! A pair of regular criminals!"

"I'm sure J. Edgar Hoover's already sent his G-men after us," I say sarcastically.

"You think so?" Frankie says.

"No, Frankie," I say. "Look, just don't tell anyone about it, okay?"

"I'll keep it on the q.t.," he says.

When we get to the park, all the kids are gathered around the baseball diamond. Frankie's team is short of players, so Frankie has me be shortstop because of my arm. He says I can throw faster than any of the boys on the field.

By the second inning we're behind by one with two outs. Frankie's on first base, and another kid, Eugene Bird, is up at bat. Eugene looks nervous; he's not a very good hitter and he almost always strikes out. Not to mention he tried to kiss me once when we were in first grade.

Eugene swings and misses the pitch.

"Strike one!" the kid who's the umpire calls.

I'm sitting on the bench waiting for my turn at bat. Most of the girls don't play anymore; they sit on the side and watch. I'm thinking about Jack Teitelzweig and wondering if maybe I should be watching games instead of playing them when a girl with blond hair held back by a light-blue head-band wearing a matching blue skirt makes her way over to where I'm sitting, trailed by two other girls. Just my luck.

"Having a nice summer, Penny?" Veronica Goodman asks with a fake smile.

I don't say anything. Mother says the only way to deal with girls like Veronica is to ignore them, although Veronica is pretty hard to ignore.

"I hear you're working at the butcher shop," she says. "Sounds like a grand time!"

The girls titter. I do my best to ignore her, watching Eugene swing too late and miss the ball again.

"Strike two!"

Poor Eugene looks like he's going to faint from all the pressure. He knows Frankie will kill him if he strikes out again. Frankie hates to lose.

Veronica leans forward and says, "So tell me. Do you get to cut up pigs all day? How exciting! What about chickens? Do you get to cut up chickens, too?"

Veronica goes on and on and on. I don't know why, but something snaps, and it's as if I turn into another person, a person with no sense at all, because I hear myself saying, "Aw, shut up already."

"What did you say?" Veronica growls.

"Nothing," I mutter.

Over on first base, Frankie's straining toward me, trying to hear what we're saying.

"My father says we should have dropped the bomb on Italy. He said it would've gotten rid of all you traitors." Her voice rises a notch. "Who do you think you are, anyway? You and your dumb cousin think you're better than us?"

"At least I'm not mean," I say before I can stop myself. Maybe I *am* spending too much time around Frankie.

Her cheeks turn hot with anger. "Well, at least *I* don't have some crazy uncle who lives in a car and wears bedroom slippers all over town."

I go cold inside.

"Your uncle is off his rocker," she says, twirling a finger by her head. "Crazy as a loon."

That's it. It's one thing to pick on me, even on Frankie, but not Uncle Dominic.

"Don't talk about my uncle," I say, standing up.

"What are you gonna do about it, huh?" she asks with a smirk.

"This," I say, and I haul off and hit her hard across the face with my fist, just the way Frankie taught me.

Veronica squeals in pain. "My nose! My nose!"

"Penny!" Frankie shouts, and starts racing across the field.

Before he gets to me, Veronica smacks me hard, right in the eye, and I stagger back, and then Frankie's leaping onto her, and the screaming begins and kids start pouring in and fists are flying and Eugene Bird doesn't have to worry if he's going to hit the ball after all, because that's the end of the game.

"I swear you do this on purpose," my mother says fiercely, jabbing my cheek with iodine.

"Ow!" I say. "That stings." What kind of nurse is she, anyhow?

"It'll hurt more if it gets infected," she says. "This is what you get for going around with that cousin of yours."

"It was Veronica! She smacked me!"

"And just look at that eye! It's going to be black by morning!"

The doorbell rings.

"That's Mr. Mulligan," she says, standing back to survey my face. "I guess there's no helping it. Go let him in. I have to check on the chicken and make sure your grandmother hasn't put her hands in it. She insisted on making her peas and onions."

Mr. Mulligan's standing on the front porch with a huge armload of cut flowers. It looks like someone died. I'm so used to seeing him holding bottles of milk that I just stare at him.

He raises his eyebrows when he sees my eye. It's all red and puffy.

"Evening, Penny," he says nervously.

He looks about as comfortable in his suit as I do in the getup Mother made me wear. I've got on a white sleeveless blouse and a checked skirt with an itchy crinoline underneath.

"These are for you," he says, handing me one of the bouquets.

I hear my mother's voice trill behind me.

"How lovely!" she says. "Wasn't that thoughtful of Mr. Mulligan, Penny?"

"Sure," I say. "Real swell."

But they're not paying any attention to me. My mother's too busy taking his hat and coat like he's the president. Mr. Mulligan gives the remaining two bouquets to my mother and Me-me, who can't get over that someone brought her flowers.

"You shouldn't have," Me-me keeps saying in a pleased voice. "No one ever brings me flowers."

"What are you talking about?" I say. "I brought you some flowers me and Frankie picked just last week!"

Me-me shoots me a disapproving look and says, "Can I get you a drink, Mr. Mulligan? Whiskey? Maybe a beer?"

"How about a glass of milk?" I suggest.

"Iced tea, if you have it," Mr. Mulligan says. "And please, call me Pat."

Me-me shoos us all into the dining room, where my mother has laid out the table with our best linen and silver and china, which we only use on holidays. This doesn't count as Christmas in my book, no sirree Bob.

Then something catches my eye. The sideboard. The wedding photograph of my mother and father is gone!

"Why don't you sit here," Me-me is saying as she ushers Mr. Mulligan to the head of the table.

My mother comes in carrying a perfect chicken, all golden brown. She's nervous, and she keeps running back into the kitchen saying she forgot to put out the butter, the rolls, the salt.

"It sure looks good," Mr. Mulligan says.

"You forgot the peas and onions," Me-me points out.

"Of course," my mother says with a forced smile. She returns a moment later with a covered dish.

"Would you carve, Pat?" Me-me asks Mr. Mulligan.

"Of course I'll carve," Pop-pop says, and picks up the knife and fork.

Mr. Mulligan looks around a little awkwardly, but nobody says anything.

"You want white meat or dark meat?" Pop-pop asks Mr. Mulligan.

"White meat, please," he says.

Pop-pop cuts off a huge chunk of dark meat and puts it on Mr. Mulligan's plate. "Here ya go, dark as night," he says.

My mother puts her hand on her forehead.

"So, Penny," Mr. Mulligan asks, "how about those Dodgers? Think they have a chance?"

"My uncle Dominic says they have a shot at the Series," I say. "My uncle Dominic, that's my father's brother, he used to play baseball in the minor leagues. He even got invited to spring training with the Dodgers."

"Your uncle sounds like an interesting fella," Mr. Mulligan says.

"He is," I tell him. "And my father was a newspaper writer."

"That's very impressive."

"You got to be really smart to be a writer. You go to college?"

Mr. Mulligan nods again, uncomfortable. "Uh—"

"Pat," my mother says in a bright voice, "can I serve you some mashed potatoes?"

"Please," Mr. Mulligan says. "You're a wonderful cook."

"Thank you," my mother says, blushing.

"I thought you said we were having steak," Pop-pop says, looking at his plate suspiciously. "This looks like chicken."

"It *is* chicken, Daddy," my mother says in exasperation.

"Wouldn't have worn a necktie if I wasn't going to get steak," he mutters to himself.

"Mr. Mulligan, would you care for some peas and onions?" I ask in a sweet voice. "Me-me's famous for her peas and onions."

Mr. Mulligan holds out his plate with a broad smile. "Why, thank you, Penny. I'd love some."

Across the table my mother shoots me a warning look, and I shrug innocently.

I give Mr. Mulligan a big helping and then watch as he takes his first bite. He blinks fast when the peas hit his tongue and then chews for a while, finally swallowing hard.

"They're delicious," he says to Me-me.

Me-me smiles happily.

"Me-me does a lot of the cooking around here," I inform Mr. Mulligan.

"Really?" he says, looking a little worried.

I wait until his plate is clean.

"More peas?" I ask.

"Uh," he says, unsure, his eyes darting between my mother and Me-me. "I don't want to eat them all."

"Please, don't be shy, there's more on the stove," Me-me says.

He holds out his plate reluctantly. "In that case, yes, please."

It takes all my willpower not to burst out laughing from the look on his face. He looks like he's going to the executioner.

"Penny," my mother says, "can you come into the kitchen for a moment, please?"

Before I can answer, Scarlett O'Hara trots over to Mr. Mulligan and calmly squats above his foot and tinkles on his shoe.

"Scarlett O'Hara!" my mother says in a horrified voice.

"Dog's bladder's going," Pop-pop says.

"Daddy!" my mother scolds.

"What? Not like it's a state secret," Pop-pop says.

"Oh, Pat, I'm so sorry," my mother says. "Here,

let me have your shoe and I'll clean it up."

Mr. Mulligan hands his shoe to my mother, who hurries into the kitchen.

Me-me stands up. "I have some rags in the basement."

Then it's just me and Pop-pop and Mr. Mulligan.

Mr. Mulligan smiles uncomfortably. He's been trying not to look at my eye the whole meal, but I know he's curious.

"That's gonna be some shiner," he says.

"Oh, this? It's nothing," I say, and lower my voice confidingly. "Mother slugged me for not making my bed. She likes things neat."

He looks at Pop-pop, as if he'll tell him it's not true. Instead, Pop-pop burps loudly.

"So, you gonna marry my daughter or what?" Pop-pop says.

Mr. Mulligan doesn't stay long. He eats the key lime pie Me-me made in two bites. When my mother asks him if he wants a second cup of coffee, he says he really needs to get home.

I wave as Mr. Mulligan's car drives away. I figure there's nothing to worry about after all.

I don't think he'll be back anytime soon.

CHAPTER TWELVE

No Poking

It's late, nearly midnight, but I can hear the soft staticky sound of the radio.

I step into my slippers and walk down the hallway to the parlor.

Pop-pop is sitting in his chair next to the radio, ear as close to it as possible, listening intently. Our radio's big, a Philco. Pop-pop's nodding like someone's talking to him, except no one's there. I stand in the doorway for a moment, watching. He doesn't notice me.

"Talking to Mickey, Pop-pop?" I ask.

He looks up, startled.

"Are you talking to Mickey?" I ask again, more loudly.

"What else would I be doing?" he barks back, and then rubs his bald head tiredly.

My grandfather thinks that his nephew, Mickey, who was killed in Germany during World War II, sometimes talks to him through the radio static. Pop-pop was heartbroken when Mickey died; he always says that Mickey was like the son he never had. There's a picture of Mickey in the upstairs hallway wearing his pilot's uniform, looking all dashing.

Pop-pop started hearing Mickey a few years ago, and at first he was real excited about it, until he told Me-me.

"You keep talking like that and they'll be sending you to the funny farm," she told him.

But sometimes he'll sneak down late at night when everyone's asleep. He maneuvers the dial back and forth, over static and music and announcers and preachers. The voices *are* kind of like ghosts, the way they come out of nowhere.

There's a hiss and Pop-pop's eyes light up.

"See?" he says excitedly. "There he is!"

All I can hear is static.

"What do you and Mickey talk about?" I ask.

"The war, of course," he says, and frowns at me. "If it weren't for all of them hooligans, he'd be alive right now. He'd be sitting right here eating a piece of your grandmother's apple pie."

Not if he was lucky, he wouldn't. Me-me's pie

is mushy and the crust is hard as a rock.

A warbling sound comes over the radio.

"What's that you say, Mickey?" Pop-pop asks loudly.

I kiss him on the head and say, "I'm going back to bed."

Me-me is standing at the top of the stairs in her bathrobe.

"He listening to that box again?" she asks.

I nod.

She shakes her head. "I just don't understand why he can't get over that boy."

The next morning when I get to the store, there's a big commotion.

"What's going on?" I ask.

"Aunt Concetta died," Frankie says with a grin.

I groan. I'm not groaning because Aunt Concetta's dead. Truth is, I didn't even know her very well. She's part of Nonny's circle of friends, these old Italian women who all wear black and play cards. She's not a real aunt, and I think she was over ninety, anyway. I groan because it means there's going to be a funeral. And a wake. And a mass.

Italians do death big. Big wakes. Big funerals. Big parties after, with lots of food. Personally, I'd rather have the party when I'm alive. What's the point in someone making you a fancy meal after you're dead? It's not like you can eat it.

But Frankie's excited.

"After this, I'll have fourteen cards!" he says.

What he's talking about is the little prayer cards you get at the funeral home when someone dies. Frankie collects them just like baseball cards. He calls them Dead Trading Cards. They're kind of like real trading cards. See, they a have a picture on one side, usually of the Virgin Mary or Jesus or one of the saints, and on the other side they have the statistics—the name of the person who died, birth and death dates, and a little prayer. Frankie's been collecting them forever, and sometimes he even trades them with other kids. I don't know about Frankie sometimes.

The evening of the wake, Me-me helps me get dressed.

"Are they expecting a lot of people?" Me-me asks as she irons what I call my funeral dress. It's black cotton with a white Peter Pan collar. It's my summer funeral dress. I have a winter funeral dress too, which I got from Uncle Nunzio. Black wool with white piping.

"Probably," I say. Usually everybody who ever

met the dead person once shows up at the funerals for my Italian relatives.

"There," she says. "That should do nicely."

I pull the dress over my head and tug it down. It feels a little tight in the chest.

"Me-me," I say, "look."

"You're growing up," Me-me says. "Take it off and I'll let out a few stitches."

A few snips and another ironing and she hands it back to me. I put it on and look at myself in the mirror. It doesn't look quite right.

"Last season for this dress," Me-me says with a critical eye.

The doorbell rings. I'm expecting Uncle Angelo, but when I open the door I see Cousin Benny standing there, tugging at his tie. I look over his shoulder and see Frankie sitting in the backseat of the car.

"What's going on? Why are you driving?"

"The baby's sick, so Aunt Teresa can't come."

"What about Uncle Angelo?"

"He's sick too," Benny says, but his mouth twitches, which means that Uncle Angelo is probably drunk again. Uncle Angelo gets "sick" a lot.

"Okay," I say, and turn to look at Me-me, who's watching me from the hall. "See you later, Me-me."

"Here," she says, handing me a white handkerchief. "A young lady should always carry one."

I sit in the front seat and look back. Frankie's wearing a suit, too tight, one of Benny's hand-me-downs from the looks of it. He's got a contented smile on his face.

"You shouldn't look so happy," I say.

"Why not?"

"Because we're going to a wake," I tell him.

Sometimes I wonder about my father's funeral. Did a lot of people show up? Did he look real handsome in the casket? Did they play all those sad hymns at the church? I would've liked to have heard Bing Crosby singing "Only Forever."

"Did you go to my father's funeral?" I ask Benny.

Benny looks over at me. He's real cute. Kind of a cuter version of Frankie, and less of a trouble-maker.

"Yeah. But I was just a kid," he says.

"What was it like?" I ask.

He grimaces. "It was terrible. Worst funeral I ever been to. Nonny tried to throw herself in the casket, and your mother, your mother . . ." His voice trails off. "Everyone was real torn up. I remember thinking, 'I never knew grown-ups could cry so much.' It was just terrible."

"Do you know how he died?"

"Didn't he have cancer?" Benny asks.

"I heard he had pneumonia," I said.

"I heard an anvil fell on him," Frankie says.

"Shut up, Frankie," Benny and I both say.

The Riggio Funeral Home is where all the wakes for the family are held. It's on the same street that Ann Marie Giaquinto lives, and Benny slows the car as we pass her house.

The funeral director, Mr. Riggio, is standing at the door greeting people.

"Hi, Mr. Riggio," I say. This is the third time we've had a funeral this year. The other two were in the spring. A lot of old people die in the spring, at least in my family. I don't think I'll ever like Easter.

"Penny," he says warmly. "You're looking lovely, sweetheart."

"Hiya, Mr. Riggio," Frankie says.

"Frankie," he says shortly, and frowns. "Everyone's in the first room, if you want to go pay your respects."

"Okay, thanks," I say.

People are lined up out into the hallway. There are rows of chairs and an aisle leading to the front of the room, where an open casket is displayed.

There are big fancy bouquets of flowers all around it. Funeral flowers are the worst, especially lilies. They always give me a headache. I don't know why they have to use the sweetest-smelling flowers to put around a dead person. Frankie says it's because dead people don't smell too good, and it helps cover up the scent.

We go inside, and Frankie grabs a bunch of the Aunt Concetta Dead Trading Cards and pockets them like they're gold. When we finally get up to the coffin, I make myself take a peek, even though I hate looking at dead bodies.

"Not bad," Frankie says.

He means it as a compliment. Aunt Concetta looks better than she did when she was alive. In fact, she looks like she's going to sit up and start talking. They've put some rouge on her and a bright-red lipstick. She was a big lady, and her cheeks are smooth because of all the fat; there's hardly a wrinkle. There's a rosary in her hands.

We kneel in front of the coffin and pretend to pray.

"You gotta kiss her," he whispers.

"I'm not kissing her," I whisper back. "You kiss her."

"What if she moves?"

"She's dead, Frankie."

"How do you know for sure? What if she's just sleeping?"

See, this is Frankie's big theory. They fix up the corpses so good that he swears they're really alive, not dead at all. He's always wanting to touch the bodies to see if they're really dead.

"We're holding up the line," I whisper, glancing back at a grumpy-looking old man who's glaring at us.

Frankie stands and leans over the coffin.

"Frankie, don't," I say. "Remember last time?"

But he just goes ahead and pokes Aunt Concetta in the arm.

"Frankie—"

He gasps. "Look, she moved!"

Behind us, the old man clears his throat loudly.

Frankie pokes Aunt Concetta again, harder this time, and the rosary beads shake a little.

Suddenly a strong arm reaches in and grabs Frankie by the scruff of the neck and me by the arm and drags us away. It's Mr. Riggio, and he's steaming mad. He hauls us out to the hallway. We're in for some trouble now!

"What did I tell you last time, Frankie Picarelli?" Mr. Riggio demands. "No poking!"

Frankie squirms in his grasp. "She moved! Honest!"

"You go near another dead body and I'm gonna bury you myself, you got me, sonny boy?" Mr. Riggio says in a hiss.

"Okay! Okay!" Frankie says, pulling away and rubbing his shoulder. "I heard you the first time."

Mr. Riggio gives Frankie a disgusted look, and me one too, and then stomps off.

"I told you not to," I say.

"Aw, simmer down. She looked alive!"

I shake my head.

"Listen, you get hit by a car and die, right? Wouldn't you want me to make sure you were really dead before they buried you?"

"I guess," I say, looking around. "Where's Benny?"

"I dunno," he says.

We wait on chairs for a while, and then the crowd starts to thin out.

Uncle Dominic catches sight of us. "You kids coming back to the house to eat?"

"Benny's supposed to be driving us," I say. "I don't know where he went."

He nods and says, "I'll take you. Come on."

As we drive down the street, Frankie points out the window. "Hey, there's Benny! And he's in a brawl!"

Sure enough, Benny is standing outside Ann

Marie Giaquinto's house, and he's fighting with her husband. Benny's taken off his suit coat, and his white shirt has blood on it. From his nose, I'm guessing. Looks like Ann Marie's husband has a pretty good right hook.

"Of all the times," Uncle Dominic mutters, and pulls over.

Frankie's leaning out the window and shouting like we're at a prizefight. "Get 'im, Benny!"

Uncle Dominic's not a big fella, but he goes right up to the two of them and says in a low voice, "That's enough of that."

Ann Marie's husband rears back, a fist raised like he's gonna pound Uncle Dominic, but Uncle Dominic just holds his ground. He stares at the fella until he lowers his hand with a curse. Ann Marie is standing at the front door, her face white as she stares at Benny.

"Why's he breaking it up?" Frankie moans in disbelief. "It was just getting good."

Uncle Dominic pushes Benny back to our car. The doors open and shut and Uncle Dominic starts the engine. I fish the hankie Me-me gave me out of my handbag and hand it to Benny, who takes it without a word. Guess she's right about always carrying one after all. Although I don't think she meant it to be for bloody noses.

"Where's your car?" Uncle Dominic asks.

"Back at Riggio's," Benny spits out.

Everyone's real quiet for a minute, and then Frankie says, "Hey, Benny, we can come back later with some other fellas and clobber him!"

"What's the matter with you?" Uncle Dominic asks Frankie.

"He's no good to her," Benny says. "He's no good at all."

"Nothing you can do about it now," Uncle Dominic tells him. "What's done is done."

"But—" Benny says.

Uncle Dominic shakes his head grimly. "Benny, there's just some things you can't change, no matter how much you want to."

No one says anything else the rest of the ride.

It's late when I get home. Pop-pop is in the parlor listening to static on the radio. I go in and sit down next to him.

"Me-me in bed?" I ask.

"Went up at eight-thirty. I don't know how that woman sleeps as much as she does. She's sleeping her life away, that's what she's doing. How was the funeral?"

"A real crowd," I say.

"Good food?"

I nod. It was.

"Mickey didn't have a great big funeral. Took too long for his body to get home. We did it real quiet-like. I drank a bottle of whiskey by myself. Mickey loved his whiskey." Pop-pop squints at me. "You know, you got Mickey's ears."

"His ears, huh?"

"He had real nice ears. Didn't stick out."

"How 'bout that," I say, and lean against Pop-pop. "Thanks for the ears, Cousin Mickey."

The static blares out of the radio, and we listen.

CHAPTER THIRTEEN

Better than Angels

The morning of my birthday is like any other. You would think me turning twelve would at least cause an earthquake, but all that happens is Scarlett O'Hara comes in and tinkles on my rug.

"Happy birthday," Me-me trills when I go into the kitchen. "I've made you banana pancakes."

"Thanks," I say as she sets a huge plate in front of me. Unfortunately, the bananas she used weren't ripe and are hard little lumps in the pancakes.

"How are they?" she asks, beaming.

"Real good," I say through a mouthful of sour pancake.

When she turns her back, I give the rest of the pancake on my plate to Scarlett O'Hara.

My mother comes into the kitchen and says, "Happy birthday, Bunny!"

She pulls a small box out from behind her back and hands it to me.

"Thanks," I say. "Can I open it now?"

"Of course," she says.

When I unwrap it, I see that it's a jewelry box. I look up at my mother, who's smiling at me. I remember her story about how she got a pearl necklace on her twelfth birthday.

"Go on," she urges me.

I carefully open the lid. Set on a bed of velvet is a ruby necklace. I recognize the ruby at once.

"It's from my engagement ring," my mother says. "I had it made into a necklace for you."

I don't know what to say.

"Do you like it?" she asks eagerly.

"Sure," I say.

"Here," she says. "Let's put it on you."

I stand still as she clasps the slender gold chain around my neck. We go to the hall and I look in the mirror, my mother standing behind me, hands on my shoulders.

"You look lovely," she says. "Just lovely."

But all I can think is that she just gave my father away.

After breakfast Frankie picks me up, and we bicycle over to the store. Uncle Ralphie's the only one there and it's quiet for once.

"Where's Aunt Fulvia?" Frankie asks.

"Took the baby to her mother's," Uncle Ralphie says, and turns to me, handing me a wrapped package. "Here you go, Princess. Happy birthday!"

It's a pecan log roll, same as every year. He gets one special for me from a friend down south.

"Thanks," I say.

"You're welcome," he says, and gives me a big hug.

"Where's my candy?" Frankie asks.

"You? All you're gonna get is a smack on the head at this rate," Uncle Ralphie says.

"I was just asking," Frankie says.

Uncle Ralphie hands us a bag of groceries. "Take this over to your grandmother's first. She wants to make one of her soups. When you get back, I'll have you stack a couple of boxes that came in this morning."

"Okay," I say.

As we bicycle over, I ask Frankie, "What'd you get me for my birthday?"

"Like I'm gonna get you anything," he says.

"Aw, come on," I say. "What did you get me?"

He pulls over and parks the bicycle. He tugs at something in his back pocket and pulls out a worn brown paper bag.

"Happy birthday," he says.

It's a crime comic, *Crime Mysteries*.

"Neat," I say. "Thanks."

"It's a good one," he says.

"You read it?"

"What?" he says. "It ain't gonna hurt it."

When we get to Nonny's house, it looks like nobody's home. Uncle Dominic's car is empty, and there are no cars in the driveway.

"Where is everybody?" I ask.

"Uncle Paulie and Aunt Gina went to Atlantic City again," he says. "I don't know where Uncle Dom is. You know him."

"I guess," I say. I have to admit, I'm a little disappointed. I kind of expected the family to do something special for my birthday.

We go around to the kitchen door and I open it.

"Surprise!"

Everyone's there—Nonny, Uncle Dominic, Uncle Nunzio, Aunt Rosa, Uncle Paulie, Aunt Gina, Uncle Angelo, Aunt Teresa, Aunt Fulvia, Uncle Sally, and all the rest of them!

Frankie slaps my shoulder, laughing. "Got you!"

Uncle Ralphie walks in the door, still wearing his apron. "Fooled you good, huh?"

"Yeah," I say, and give him a big hug. "You fooled me, all right. Who's at the store?"

He waves his hand at me. "Closed."

"You're only gonna be twelve once," Uncle Sally says.

Uncle Paulie pats Frankie on the head. "It was your no-good cousin's idea to have everyone park down the street to throw you off the scent. A regular criminal mastermind, our Frankie."

"I'm good!" Frankie protests.

"Yeah, good at sneaking around." Uncle Paulie lowers his voice. "I better not catch you digging in the yard, you got me?"

"Who said anything about digging?" Frankie says, all innocence.

"It's time for the birthday girl to blow out her candles," Aunt Gina declares, carrying in a cake.

The cake is huge. It's got pecan icing, and in white piping it says "Happy Birthday, Princess!"

"It's a rum cake," Uncle Nunzio says with a wink. "You're a big girl now."

Uncle Dominic whistles, and Queenie V trots over. He starts singing "Happy Birthday to You" and Queenie V gets all excited and starts running in circles, her head in the air, yipping and howling along with Uncle Dominic so that it sounds like *she's* the one singing! When the dog's finished, everyone claps and shouts, "Encore!" and she does it again. Uncle Dominic kneels down and gives her a biscuit.

"Gosh, that was something else," I say, laughing. "Was that what you've been trying to teach her all this time?"

Uncle Dominic nods. "I tried to teach her 'Pennies from Heaven,' but she couldn't get the hang of it."

I lean over to blow out the candles.

"Make a wish," Uncle Dominic tells me.

But I don't know what to wish for. I have everything I want.

After we eat the cake, we go into the dining room, where a huge lunch has been laid out. All my favorites: potato croquettes, rice balls, cold stuffed peppers, eggplant, lasagna, and *pastiera*—the whole works.

"Your grandmother's been cooking for days," Uncle Paulie says.

"*Tesoro mio,*" Nonny says. "*Ti voglio bene.*"

I know these words.

"I love you, too, Nonny," I say back.

Pretty soon everyone's eating. I'm allowed a thimbleful of Chianti, and between that and the rum cake, I'm feeling giddy.

Frankie whispers into my ear, "I think Uncle Paulie's onto us. About the backyard and all."

They pass presents down the long length of the table. Uncle Nunzio and Aunt Rosa give me a fancy satin skirt, and Uncle Angelo and Aunt Teresa give me a brush and comb set, and Aunt Gina and Uncle Paulie give me a pair of black patent Mary Janes.

"Dancing shoes," Aunt Gina says, grinning.

Nonny gives me a lace collar she's made, and Uncle Sally gives me five dollars.

"Buy something you want, sweetheart," he says.

After all this, Uncle Nunzio wheels in a brand-new shiny bicycle with a big red bow. Frankie gives a low whistle.

"We heard your old bicycle had an accident," Uncle Nunzio says.

"Gosh," I say, stunned. "That's a swell bicycle."

Baby Enrico toddles over to the bicycle and waves at it and says, "Carry you! Carry you!"

Uncle Nunzio lifts him up on the seat, and Enrico gives a big grin and everyone laughs.

"Better watch that kid," Frankie says under his breath.

"There's one more present," someone says, and I look up to see Uncle Dominic standing in the doorway. Naturally, he hasn't joined us for lunch.

"There's more?" I ask.

He passes a small envelope down the table. I'm thinking maybe it's money, but when I look inside, I can't believe what I'm seeing.

"What is it, doll?" Aunt Gina asks.

"Tickets," I say slowly, looking up to meet Uncle Dominic's eyes, "to the Dodgers game tonight!"

"You're going to the game?" Frankie bursts out.

I look at Uncle Dominic.

"An old pal of mine at the ball club got 'em for me," he explains.

"Hey, what about me?" Frankie asks. "Did you get me a ticket?"

"This is the Princess's day," Uncle Nunzio tells him.

Frankie glowers. "Yeah, well, I better get tickets on my birthday, that's all I'm saying."

"I got you a ticket too, Frankie," Uncle Dominic says, shaking his head.

Frankie's face brightens. "You hear that, Penny? We're going to the game!"

Uncle Dominic looks at me and says, "Whaddya say, Princess?"

Uncle Dominic and Frankie wait in the car while I run into the house.

Mother's standing on a ladder in the middle of the parlor with a garland of crepe paper. There are balloons everywhere, and the dining room table has presents on it.

"Daddy," she's saying, "lift the paper higher."

"What?" Pop-pop asks. "What?"

My mother sees me standing in the doorway and freezes. "Bunny, what are you doing home so early?"

"Um, is this for me?"

"Of course," she says with a smile. "Although it was supposed to be a surprise."

"I'm surprised," I tell her.

She climbs down off the ladder. "Maybe you should go out and come back in a few hours. Act surprised."

"Look," I say, waving the Dodgers tickets. "Tickets to the Dodgers game tonight. Uncle Dominic got 'em for me."

She goes still. "Did he?"

Outside, Frankie leans on the horn.

"Me-me made a special dinner," my mother says. "And a cake, too."

"Please," I say. "Please."

My mother glances at Uncle Dominic's car idling at the curb. Some emotion flits across her face, and she closes her eyes briefly. When she opens them, she seems resigned.

"Very well," she says. "You can go."

I fling myself at her and give her a big hug.

"Thank you!" I say. "This is the best present ever!"

She smiles a little sadly. "We'll eat your cake for breakfast."

"For breakfast," I promise.

Even though I've lived not far from New York City my whole life, I've never actually been. Mother's always said that the city isn't safe, which must mean it's pretty exciting.

Uncle Dominic drives us through the city so we can see the sights. It's incredible! The buildings are so tall that I have to crane my neck to see the tops of them. We drive by Radio City Music Hall and Grand Central Station and the Empire State Building and finally downtown over the bridge into Brooklyn.

The Dodgers are playing at their home ball-park, Ebbets Field. It takes a while, but we finally find a parking spot and follow the crowd. Everybody's talking and cheering. There's such a feeling of excitement in the air, like nothing I've ever felt before. It seems like the whole city is going to the game.

A couple of boys are talking to a policeman at the gate.

"You gotta let us in," one of the boys is saying. "Look, our buddy here got crippled by polio. He ain't got nothing to look forward to but baseball."

"Yeah," the crippled boy says, waving a crutch. "I ain't got nothing but Dem Bums now."

The policeman studies the crippled boy and shakes his head and says, "Aw, go on in. You're breaking my heart."

The kids grin at each other and slide through the gate.

"I'm gonna have to try that sometime," Frankie says, impressed. "Just need to find a crippled kid."

We go into the rotunda. I've heard a lot about this rotunda. It's one thing to hear it described but another to see it with your own eyes. The rotunda is marble decorated with baseball stitching. There are gilded ticket windows, and the lights are shaped like baseballs held up by baseball bats.

"It's beautiful," I say.

"Wait until you see this," Uncle Dominic says, and I follow him through a gate.

My eyes go wide in shock as I get my first look at Ebbets Field. The diamond is a brilliant green, and there are signs all along the walls by the score-board.

Frankie's looking at a sign. "What's that mean? 'Hit Sign, Win Suit.'"

"That's Abe Stark, kid," a fella next to us says. "Any ballplayer who hits that sign gets a free suit. Abe Stark's got a shop on Pitkin Avenue."

"Bet I could hit that sign," Frankie says, sizing it up.

"See that?" Uncle Dominic says, pointing at a big sign for Schaefer beer on top of the right-center-field scoreboard. "The *H* will light up for a hit and the *E* for an error," he says.

I'm expecting we'll be sitting way up high, which is where it seems like most of the people are going, but Uncle Dominic just heads straight to the front row along the first-base line, right above the dugout for the Dodgers. We're so close to the field, we can almost reach out and touch the ballplayers.

Then Uncle Dominic slides down the row and sits down.

"We're sitting here?" I ask, astonished.

Uncle Dominic nods.

Frankie leans over the front rail. "Hey! That's Jackie Robinson! He's right there! Hey, Jackie!" he hollers.

They're all there—Pee Wee Reese and Duke Snider and Gil Hodges and Roy Campanella!

The organist, Gladys Gooding, bangs out "Follow the Dodgers" and the game gets under way. It feels more like a carnival than a ball game. There's so much to look at and hear. Men hawking hot dogs and cold beer chant, "Getcha cold one now, heah dey are, cold as da Nawt Pole." The Brooklyn Dodgers Sym-phony Band plays "Three Blind Mice" when the umpires come out, and a funny woman sitting in the bleachers named Hilda Chester rings her cowbell and shouts, "Eatcha heart out, ya bum!"

We sit in the best seats in the house, and I don't even have to look up at the sky to know that this is better than anything the angels can offer.

CHAPTER FOURTEEN

All for the Best

A few days later I wake up and there's a bad smell in the air.

At first I think the toilet is leaking, but then I look down and see Scarlett O'Hara lying on the rug next to my bed right in her own mess.

She blinks up at me and whines.

"Scarlett O'Hara," I say. "Not again."

I step over her and go to the bathroom for a towel. When I get back, she's still lying there.

"Scarlett, come here," I say, kneeling down next to her.

She scrabbles with her front paws, but something's wrong, because she can't move her back legs and she looks kind of confused. That's when I notice her tail isn't moving either. I pick her up gently and wipe her off and then wrap her in the towel and carry her into the kitchen.

Me-me's sitting at the table, sipping coffee.

"Good morning," she says, and then sees the tears streaming down my cheeks. "What's the matter?"

"I think Scarlett O'Hara's hurt," I say. "She can't move her back legs."

"Oh, Penny," she says.

I go into the parlor and call the store. Uncle Ralphie picks up on the other end.

"Uncle Ralphie," I say, "I can't come to work. I gotta take Scarlett O'Hara to the veterinarian. She's sick."

"Sorry to hear that, sweetheart," he says, but there's a rushed sound to his voice. "Say, you seen Frankie lately?"

"No," I say.

"If you see him, you tell him to give me a call, all right?"

"Is something wrong?" I ask.

"Nothing for you to worry about, sweetheart," he says. "You just take care of your dog."

"Okay," I say, hanging up the phone.

When we get back from the veterinarian, Me-me goes down to the basement and finds my old cloth diapers from back when I was a baby.

"Use these," she tells me.

Scarlett O'Hara's real good when I put the diaper on her.

"Dog ain't well?" Pop-pop asks gruffly.

I don't bother to put up a brave front. "Dr. Brogan says she's real sick. He says to just make her comfortable."

Pop-pop looks thoughtful. "Best thing for her."

I take her dog bed out to the summer porch and place her in it so that she has a nice view of the yard. I sit next to her, brushing her fur. She whines softly at the squirrels running around in her backyard. I'm tempted to go out and chase them away myself, seeing as she can't do it.

"Feeling better, Scarlett?" I ask, patting her fur.

I see a flurry of movement in the bushes out back.

"*Pssst!*" the bushes say. "Penny!"

At first I think maybe I'm losing my marbles, but then I see a hand wave at me from behind the biggest bush. I walk out into the yard, and when I reach the bush, the hand grabs me and pulls me behind it.

It's Frankie. He's dirty, and his clothes look like he slept in them. He starts talking fast, and he's not making any sense at all.

"The police been here?"

"Police?"

"Yeah," he says, looking around nervously. "You seen any?"

"What are you talking about? And why are you hiding in the bushes?"

"I been waiting for you all morning," he says.

"Why didn't you come through the front door, then?" I ask.

"'Cause people are looking for me," he says in a low voice.

My stomach sinks. "Frankie, what did you do?"

He closes his eyes and swallows. "I figured I'd just, you know, borrow some money from the collection. Help out at home."

"You robbed St. Anthony's?"

"I was gonna give it back! Honest! But when Father Giovanni came in, I panicked. It was dark, and I knocked over this bookshelf and all these hymnals fell on him."

"Was he hurt?"

He shakes his head. "Nah, but I don't think he's too happy about the window."

"The window?"

"I smashed a window to get out."

"Uncle Ralphie's looking for you," I tell him.

"I'm a wanted man!" he says wildly.

"Frankie, you're just a kid. They can't send you to jail. We'll tell them it was an accident."

There's a dull look in his eye. "Guess I should just turn myself in."

"You can stay in the basement," I say quickly. "No one will ever know."

He shrugs, resigned already. "They'll find me here. First place they'll look."

We both stand there for a minute.

"Come inside," I say. "We'll call Uncle Ralphie. He'll know what to do."

Frankie hesitates and then nods.

"Where'd you sleep, anyhow?" I ask.

"Behind that bush," he says, scratching his arm fiercely. "You got some mean ants back there."

We go onto the porch and Scarlett O'Hara lifts her head.

"Why's she wearing a diaper?" he asks. "You playing house or something?"

"She's sick," I say. "She can't move her back legs."

He kneels down and scratches her on the chin. "Scarlett, don't let no cats see you in these diapers.

You'll be the laughingstock of the neighborhood."

"The doctor said she might die," I whisper.

"You can't give up on her," Frankie says sharply, looking up at me. "You can't never give up on someone, even if they are a dog, right, Scarlett?"

Scarlett O'Hara whines low in her throat as if she couldn't agree more.

"What's going to happen?" I ask Mother that night at dinner.

Uncle Ralphie picked up Frankie and took him down to the police station. "He'll probably have to go to reform school, Bunny. You can't just go around robbing churches."

I want to shout and say it's not his fault, that he was just trying to help out.

"You know I never liked you spending so much time with him," she says. "He's been in and out of trouble for years."

"Like father, like son," Me-me says, shaking her head. "That whole family has more trouble with the law than—"

"Mother," my mother snaps, cutting her off.

Me-me purses her lips.

"Frankie's not a criminal," I say.

"He is now," my mother says.

"He's my cousin!" I say.

But when I look around the table, no one will meet my eyes.

After lunch, I go over to Frankie's house.

I ring the doorbell but nobody answers. I can hear the baby screaming inside, so I ring again.

"Who is it?" Aunt Teresa shouts through the door.

"It's me, Aunt Teresa. Penny."

The door opens abruptly. Aunt Teresa has baby Michael in her arms, and there are bags under her eyes.

"Is Frankie home?" I ask.

"Frankie!" she hollers, and walks away.

Frankie comes to the door, and he looks terrible.

"You okay?" I ask.

"I'm sunk," he says. "They're gonna send me away."

"But don't you get a trial? You have to tell them why you did it!"

He shrugs. "It won't matter with this judge. He told me last time he'd better not see me in his courtroom again."

"There's gotta be something we can do," I tell him, but his face looks defeated.

"Frankie!" Aunt Teresa calls. "Get in here, now!"

"We'll figure something out," I say urgently. "You know—"

"I better go," he says in a tired voice, and shuts the door.

When I get home, Pop-pop's waiting for me on the porch. He puts a hand on my shoulder and looks down at me.

"Scarlett O'Hara" is all he says.

My mother comes into my room when she gets home from work. I've never actually seen her cry, but she doesn't look too good. Her eyes are red and she's real pale.

"Pop-pop just told me about Scarlett O'Hara," she says, and chokes. "She was such a good dog. I had her before I had you, you know."

"My father gave her to you, right?" I ask.

"Yes," she says, and looks past me, at the wall. "It was probably for the best. This way she didn't suffer long. At least she died at home, surrounded by people who love her."

That night as I lie in bed, all I can think is how none of this is for the best. How is Scarlett O'Hara dying and Frankie going to reform school good for anyone?

I imagine Frankie in some horrible boys' home on a cold iron bed, and I know for certain that if he goes in there, he'll come out bad. That he'll never survive something like that—there's just no way. He's like a tree that's got a crack in it.

One good storm and he'll fall right over.

The next morning I go to Nonny's. Uncle Dominic's sitting in his car, doing a crossword puzzle. I slide into the front seat.

"You gotta help Frankie," I tell him. "You can't let them send him away."

"I don't know what I can do, Princess," he says.

"But the police don't know the real story! Uncle Angelo lost his job again and they need money, and he was just going to borrow it. Frankie's not a criminal! He was just trying to help."

Uncle Dominic doesn't say anything.

"Please," I plead, and my voice is getting louder, higher. "You know Frankie. Why won't anyone stand up for him?"

"Princess—"

I'm crying now. "He's just a kid! He's my best friend! And Scarlett O'Hara's dead, and everyone keeps saying it's all for the best, but it's not! It's not!"

And then Uncle Dominic is wrapping his arms around me and letting me sob into his shirt.

"It'll be okay, Princess," he says again and again. "It'll be okay."

Frankie comes over to my house that afternoon.

"It's all over! I ain't going away!" he says.

"Really?"

He nods and I'm so happy that I just hug him. He tolerates it for a brief moment before pushing me away.

"Aw, c'mon already," he says. "You're worse than Nonny."

"So what happened?" I ask.

"Way I hear it, Uncle Dominic talked to Uncle Nunzio, and Uncle Nunzio is buddies with the bishop, and the bishop agreed to drop the charges."

"That's great," I say. "So you won't get into any trouble?"

"Nah," he says, and then frowns. "But Uncle Nunzio said I'm going to have to work at the factory to pay for a new window at St. Anthony's. And I have to apologize to Father Giovanni." He looks a little glum. "I don't think I'm gonna be an altar boy anymore."

"It could be worse, right?"

He smiles then, the first smile I've seen since all this happened. "Guess what! Uncle Nunzio told Pop he has a friend who's looking for someone to drive a truck and did he want the job and Pop said yes! Ain't that great?"

"That's swell," I say, even though I know it won't last. Still, I don't want to say anything that will take that smile off his face.

He suddenly notices that the dog bed is empty. "Say, how's Scarlett?"

I don't say anything; I just look at him.

"Aw, geez," he says. "Some rotten week, huh?"

"And how."

"Where'd you put her?" he asks.

"Pop-pop said she'd keep better in the basement until we bury her. I don't know where she should go."

Frankie's face lights up.

"I know the perfect place," he says.

I ask Mother, and I'm surprised when she says it's all right.

Uncle Dominic digs a grave for Scarlett O'Hara in Nonny's backyard, right next to where all the Kings and Queenies are buried. Our cousin Sister Laura comes over to Nonny's and says a prayer over the grave, and Frankie puts the record player in the window and plays Bing Crosby singing "Here Lies Love." It's not Shady Grove, but it's real nice.

"She'll have lots of company," Uncle Dominic says to me after he's finished patting down the earth.

"Yeah," I say, and feel a little better.

That night when I go to sleep, I dream of Scarlett O'Hara with all the Kings and Queenies. She's chasing them around, nipping at their heels, squirrels running everywhere.

The happiest dog in all of Heaven.

CHAPTER FIFTEEN

A Punishment
Worse than Death

It's a steamy August day.

After we finish work at the store, we bicycle back to my house for lunch. It's so hot that I'm soaked straight through and go change into a fresh blouse and a pair of pedal pushers.

When I come out, Frankie's sitting in the kitchen with Pop-pop, eating one of Me-me's liverwurst sandwiches. He must be pretty desperate:

"Say, you ever get to use those bazooka guns?" Frankie is asking Pop-pop. "I tell ya, if I ran into a Jap or a Nazi, I'd use a bazooka gun on him! *Bam!*"

I don't know who's worse, Frankie or Pop-pop.

"What?" Pop-pop says. "What'd you say?"

"I said, 'Did you get to use those bazooka guns?'" Frankie shouts.

"Why you want to know? You planning on shooting someone?" Pop-pop asks suspiciously.

"Nah," Frankie says. "Give me a hymnal any day."

"Frankie!" I say.

"My nephew, Mickey, was a pilot in the war," Pop-pop says. "Air force."

"Like Gregory Peck in *Twelve O'Clock High?*" Frankie asks.

Pop-pop nods.

"I like Gregory Peck," I say. "He sure is handsome."

"When Mickey told me he was going over to Europe, I said, 'Mickey, eat as much as you can,'" Pop-pop says.

"Why'd you tell him that?" Frankie asks.

"'Cause that way if he got shot down and captured by the Nazis, he wouldn't starve to death."

"Good advice. So'd he get shot down or what?"

"Over Germany. Didn't survive the crash." Pop-pop's voice breaks, and his eyes get all watery. "Sticks in my craw just thinking about it."

"Guess he didn't have to worry about starving," Frankie says under his breath.

Pop-pop sees Frankie and me staring at him and shakes himself and says, "Go on. Don't you have someplace to go? Stop bothering me."

We grab our sandwiches and head out to the front porch.

"What do you wanna do?" I ask, looking up at the hot sun beating down.

"Go ask Me-me if you can go to the pool," Frankie says.

"Esther Williams would have to show up and personally invite me before I'd be allowed to stick my big toe in the pool," I say.

Like I said, some people think you can catch polio from swimming in public pools and one of them is my mother, which is why I haven't set foot in a pool all summer. My mother tells me all the terrible stories about what it's like to have polio; how the kids who get it have to stay in an iron lung and are crippled and even die. Far as I can tell, the only thing nursing school did for my mother was scare her about everything.

"Go on," Frankie says. "Ask her. Me-me's a softy. Maybe she'll let you go."

Me-me's paying bills when I go inside.

"May I go to the pool?" I ask. "Please?"

She shakes her head. "You want to end up in an iron lung?"

So much for her being a softy.

"It can't be hotter in an iron lung than it is here," I mutter, and go back outside.

"Well?" Frankie asks.

"At this rate, I'll be a hundred before I get to see the inside of a swimming pool," I say.

We sit on the porch and play cards in the shade. Frankie's the better card player, mostly because he cheats. His father taught him all sorts of card tricks that he learned when he was away in jail.

"Knock it off already," I say after he wins the fifth hand in a row.

"What?" he says, all innocence.

I give him a look. "I saw you pull that card out of your pocket."

"What card?"

"The ace," I say.

"You're just a sore loser," he says with a small snicker.

"Am not."

Me-me comes out wearing a hat, Pop-pop at her side.

"We're going over to see the Harts," she announces. "We won't be back until five o'clock."

"Okay," I say.

She eyes Frankie. "You'll be all right here on your own?"

"Yes, Me-me," I say. "I promise not to do anything exciting."

She presses her lips together as if she's unsure about leaving me with Frankie.

"What're we waiting for? My hair to grow back?" Pop-pop asks.

"Don't get into trouble," Me-me calls over her shoulder as they walk to the car.

The minute the car's disappeared around the corner, Frankie grabs my hand and says, "Let's go!"

"Go where?" I ask.

He screws up his face. "The pool! Where else?"

"But Me-me said I can't go."

Frankie has a devilish gleam in his eye. "Just think of all that nice cool water going to waste."

I hesitate. "I don't know."

"Come on," Frankie says. "We go now and get back before Me-me and Pop-pop return, see?"

I look at him uncertainly. "What if my mother finds out?"

He winks at me. "She'll never know."

I'm floating on my back, looking up at the blue sky, a smile on my face.

After changing into our suits and grabbing towels, we rode our bicycles over to the pool. It seems like every kid in town is here today. I guess the other mothers don't share my mother's worries. Either that or they can't take their kids' whining.

But the biggest surprise of the afternoon is finding out that Jack Teitelzweig is a junior lifeguard here!

"Hi, Penny," Jack says.

I'm so startled, I don't know what to say; I just sort of nod at him. Luckily he can't see my horrible hair because I'm wearing a bathing cap.

Now I can't stop thinking about Jack. He's got an awfully nice smile. All of a sudden I'm having these crazy ideas about Jack asking me on a date or taking me to a dance. I almost blush when I imagine what it would be like to kiss him. Then I realize I really must be dreaming because I hear Jack calling my name.

"Penny," he calls.

I just keep floating, but he calls my name again, and this time I open my eyes.

"Penny Falucci. Please come to the lifeguard stand," he calls through the bullhorn.

I can't believe my ears, but when I look up, I see Jack standing at the side of the pool waving at me. I wave back at him and then freeze. Because standing right next to him is . . .

My mother.

All the kids in the pool start laughing and clapping, and a few even whistle as I make my way over. Veronica's sitting on the side and gives me a little wave.

And that's when I know for certain that ending up in an iron lung can't possibly be any worse than dying of pure embarrassment.

My mother lectures me the whole way to the house. Apparently, she came home early to surprise me, but when she couldn't find me, she got suspicious.

"I am so disappointed," she says. "Wait till Meme hears about this little stunt of yours."

I don't say anything; I just stare straight ahead.

"This is what we get for trusting you to behave? To do the right thing?" she demands.

"An iron lung can't be any worse than living like this!" I shout. "I can't go to the movies! I can't go in the pool! It's like I'm a prisoner! You won't let me do anything!"

"We'll see about that," she says grimly.

I'm not allowed to leave the house for the rest of the summer, and it's only the beginning of August. The only places I can go are the store and Nonny's house.

"How was I supposed to know she'd have a spy?" Frankie protests when he finds out.

After spending the morning at the store, I go straight home and make myself a cream cheese and grape jelly sandwich and go out to the front porch to eat it. This is the most exciting my day will get. It's only been a week, but I can honestly say I know what it feels like to be in jail. No wonder Uncle Angelo is such a wreck. How can anyone do anything after such torture?

Me-me opens the front door and smiles. "Would you like some cake?"

I shake my head.

"Maybe we can make a new bedspread for your room this afternoon," she suggests. "You've been saying you wanted something different."

"It doesn't matter anymore."

Me-me sighs and closes the door reluctantly.

I know Me-me is trying to cheer me up, but a new bedspread isn't going to make up for the plain fact that my life is ruined. Every other kid in town is having a great time, and I'm stuck at home with Me-me and Pop-pop. I have weeks of this to look forward to, not to mention all the teasing I'm going to get when I go back to school. And that's not the end of it. Mother's dating Mr. Mulligan again! I thought I'd gotten rid of him, but he showed up at the door last night.

"You're going out with him again?" I asked my mother. "But he's, he's—"

"Not another word from you, young lady," she snapped. "I haven't forgotten your little performance when he came over for dinner."

While I'm considering whether or not I should just run away to Alaska because at least it's cool there, a car pulls up.

"Hey, Princess," Uncle Dominic calls through the open window.

I run to the car.

"Hi!" I say, leaning in.

"You busy?"

"Not unless you count sitting around doing nothing," I say.

"What do you say to going to the beach?" he asks.

My face falls. "I can't. I got in trouble."

"I heard," he says.

I look down at the ground, and then my head snaps up when I hear him say, "Maybe I can talk to your grandmother."

"Really? You would do that for me?"

He bites his lip and nods.

I wait on the porch while he's inside talking to Me-me. I'll never know what he told her; all I know is that a few minutes later she comes out to the porch.

"Be home by dinner and don't spoil your appetite," she says.

I can't believe my ears. "Really?"

Me-me's face turns serious. "If your mother finds out about this . . ."

I hug her soft waist and say the words that got me into this fix to begin with.

"She'll never know."

The beach is already crowded by the time we get there, but we find a good spot just the same. Uncle Dominic's made a real effort to be normal, and I know it's for me. He's not wearing slippers, just regular shoes and bathing trunks.

I don't know if it's because we're out of the neighborhood, but he seems like a different man, happier. He runs straight out into the ocean, diving beneath a big wave and popping up on the other side. We bob in the waves with the rest of the kids and parents on vacation. Some of the fathers look sort of stunned, like they can't believe they're in the ocean, their toes brushing the sand, and not in some factory or office somewhere.

"Watch out for the sharks," Uncle Dominic says, baring his teeth. He has a chip in his front tooth.

We swim until we're tired, and then we go and lie on the beach to dry off. Uncle Dominic buys us a bag of peanuts from the man walking around. Some young ladies have put their blankets next to ours. They're pretty, and they're looking at Uncle Dominic like he's saltwater taffy.

I don't usually think of Uncle Dominic as the eligible-bachelor type, but here on the beach, out of the back room of the store, I see what they see: he's got a real sweet smile. He seems like a normal fella at the beach, but it's just like a pool of water in the desert: a mirage.

I hear the young ladies invite him to have a drink with them up on the boardwalk.

"Some other time," he says. "I have a date with my niece here."

"Your niece, how sweet," the young ladies coo.

We change into our clothes and head to the boardwalk.

"How about those rides?" he asks with a grin, and I grin right back at him.

We go to the bumper cars first, my favorite. Then there's the Ferris wheel, the teacups, the Tilt-A-Whirl, and the whip. Afterward we sit on a bench on the boardwalk and eat hot dogs with sauerkraut and wash them down with fresh-squeezed orangeade, the coldest, most delicious drink in the whole world. Uncle Dominic buys me a coconut patty to eat on the ride home and it melts in my mouth.

We've got the windows rolled down and Bing Crosby's singing "A Perfect Day" on the radio. As we drive down my street, I look over at Uncle Dominic. For a moment I imagine that he is my father and it's just the two of us, coming home after a day at the beach. Something any regular kid would do.

We pull up in front of my house. My mother's car isn't there yet.

"It was a perfect day, huh, Princess?" he asks, and pulls out his handkerchief, swiping a smear of mustard off my cheek.

I watch his car drive away and can't help but think Bing and my uncle Dominic were both right.

It was a pretty perfect day.

CHAPTER SIXTEEN

So This Is Heaven

Me and Frankie are in the basement of Nonny's house.

Frankie's got his heart set on finding Grandpa Falucci's treasure, and he's got a new theory about where it's buried.

"What if Uncle Sally had it all wrong? What if Grandpa put it 'underground' and not 'in the ground'? What if it's in the basement?" Frankie says.

So now Frankie's been sneaking down here every chance he gets, which isn't very often because Nonny's almost always cooking. But this morning Frankie volunteered us to do the laundry so Uncle Paulie could take Nonny and Aunt Gina to Uncle Nunzio's factory to get new coats. Uncle

Dominic's napping in his car, so the coast is clear.

Frankie's across the room, teetering on top of a shaky-looking ladder, studying a brick near the ceiling while I feed wet clothes through the wringer.

"Looks sort of loose," he says, but I'm not really listening to him; I have too much on my mind.

This morning I had a fight with Me-me. We were sitting at the breakfast table eating watery scrambled eggs when she told me that Mr. Mulligan was coming over for dinner tonight.

"Again?" I asked.

"He's a nice man," she said.

"He's boring."

"Young lady," Me-me said, her tone sharp.

"What do we need him for, anyway?" I asked.

"You need a man in your life," she said.

"I have Uncle Dominic and Uncle Paulie and Uncle Ralphie and—"

"Your mother needs a husband," she said flatly. "She's been alone for a long time. You think it's been easy for her?"

"But why him?" I demanded. "I don't want him for my father."

"He's not going to be if you keep this up," she said under her breath.

Across the room, Frankie gives a low whistle. "This brick is a different color than the other ones, like it was replaced or something."

"I could use some help, you know," I say loudly. "I'm the only one doing any laundry here."

"Aw, knock it off already," he says. "We find the loot, and you can hire someone to do the wash."

"But isn't it stealing?" I ask.

Frankie turns on me with a scowl. "It's not stealing if nobody knows about it. Besides, you think Grandpa would want all this money just going to waste here?"

"I guess not," I say.

As I feed a wet slip into the wringer, I start thinking about what's going to happen if my mother marries Mr. Mulligan. What then? Will I have to call him Daddy?

I can already tell Mother is getting different. I lost the lucky bean somewhere in the house and was up late last night looking for it, and she didn't even help me look!

"You want me to have bad luck?" I asked her.

"That's all just superstitious nonsense anyway, Penny," she said.

Frankie's yelp of excitement startles me.

"Holy smoke!" he shouts. "Penny! Look!"

I turn as Frankie pulls a cigar box from a hole

high in the wall. A waterfall of loose dirt and old cement rains down on his head. He opens it and gasps, teetering on the ladder. The box goes flying into the air, and bills start fluttering out like butterflies set free. It must be a million bucks, there's so much money everywhere, and I'm thinking that this is a miracle or something when I feel a tug on my fingers.

My right arm's yanked, and when I look back, I see it being pulled through the wringer. I try to scream, but all that comes out is a wheeze like Scarlett O'Hara used to make when you stepped on her tail. I can't believe what I'm seeing, 'cause I can't. I mean, that mangled thing caught in the wringer can't be part of me, 'cause if it was, wouldn't I be feeling some pain or something. And that's when it hits me, the pain, like a shot, and I yell, I yell, "Frankie! Frankie! Frankie!" and he comes running over, his face white as snow. He just stands there staring in disbelief.

My right arm has been pulled through the wringer all the way up to my armpit and it's stuck, but the wringer's still going, grinding down on my arm, like Uncle Dominic making ground beef.

"Make it stop!" I scream.

Frankie jumps to life and pulls the plug out of the wall, and I feel a jolt as it stops.

For a moment we both just stare at my arm stuck in the wringer, and when I meet Frankie's eyes, he's got the same look he had that morning he showed up in my backyard, and I know it's bad, it's terrible, it's horrible, it's the end.

All at once the pain washes over me, and I start to scream, my voice loud—I never knew I had a voice this loud—and I'm screaming, "Get it out! Get it out!" and Frankie's saying, "It'll be okay! It'll be okay!" but I just scream and scream and he's running upstairs, shouting for Uncle Dominic.

Then I'm all alone in the basement, money littering the floor, and everything slows down so that my whole life, my whole world, is reduced to this moment, this wringer, this arm that used to be an arm that I can't imagine will ever hold a lucky bean or a baseball or an ice cream cone or anything at all, ever again.

Frankie comes running back with Uncle Dominic and they get my arm out of the wringer, but by the time they do, I'm done with screaming, I'm all screamed out, and all I can do is moan low in my throat. When Uncle Dominic picks me up to carry me upstairs, the sudden jolting makes me throw up the scrambled eggs from breakfast, and then everything goes black for a moment.

I blink my eyes open, and Uncle Dominic is leaning over me and I'm laying across the front seat of his car, the wheels rumbling beneath my head, my arm wrapped in what looks like the white lacy tablecloth from the dining room table, and then I realize that all the red on it is my blood.

"Hang on, Princess. We're almost at the hospital," Uncle Dominic says urgently.

But his face changes, and it's not Uncle Dominic anymore; the face looking down at me is younger, the jaw thinner, the eyes darker.

"My Penny," my father says, leaning down, touching my forehead, his hand soft as an angel's. "*Cocca di papà.*"

And that's when I know I'm dying.

The best thing about dying, I decide, is that I'm finally going to get to see my father. He'll be waiting for me, I'll have a ticker-tape parade, and there'll be butter pecan ice cream. I can already see Scarlett O'Hara yipping around, trying to bite my ankles and tinkling all over the clouds. We'll go for a nice long swim in the big pool and maybe take in a movie. Then we'll go see a Dodgers game.

But when I open my eyes, there's no ice cream or ticker tape, just a terrible numb feeling on the right side of my body and the sound of yelling, like someone's having a boxing match. I half expect to see some fella selling peanuts and taking bets.

Except the voice doing the shouting is my mother's.

"You were supposed to watch her!" she's shouting. "You were supposed to watch her!"

I hear Uncle Nunzio's voice, the same steady voice he uses when he talks to his customers.

"Ellie," he says, "it was an accident. It's not Dominic's fault—"

"Don't you talk to me about accidents!" she shrieks wildly. "He killed Freddy and now he's almost killed my daughter!"

"Ellie, don't," Uncle Paulie pleads. "Please don't."

I open my eyes to see the room crowded with people—it seems like everyone's here. There's Frankie and Uncle Paulie and Aunt Gina and Uncle Nunzio and Aunt Rosa and Me-me and Pop-pop and Nonny. In the middle of the room my mother and Uncle Dominic are standing across from each other like boxers in a ring.

"Ellie," Uncle Dominic says in a choked voice.

But it's too much for my mother somehow, and she takes two steps until she's standing in front of him, and she slaps him, slaps him so hard, I'm sure they hear it in New York City.

The whole room gasps, and Mother raises her hand again.

Uncle Dominic blanches, like he's been sucker punched, but he doesn't say anything; he just stands there, waiting for the next blow to fall. He looks terrible. His shirt is stained under the armpits, and my blood's on it too, and I can't take it, I can't take seeing that horrible look in his eyes, like he wishes he was dead and my mother is his executioner. My two favorite people standing there, hating each other.

"Stop," I say. It comes out as a croak.

My mother whirls around, her face white, and she is at my side in two steps, her hand on my forehead, saying, "My baby, my baby."

Behind her I see Uncle Dominic's eyes close, and then Uncle Nunzio starts shooing everyone out.

"Leave them be," Uncle Nunzio says.

When it's only me and Mother and Me-me and Pop-pop, the doctor comes in.

"I'm Dr. Goldstein," he says.

Dr. Goldstein kind of looks like Gregory Peck, except that he's wearing a white coat and a stethoscope. He's got those movie-star good looks: the greased-back hair, the sparkly smile. He looks too handsome to be a doctor, and the first words out of my mouth are "*You're* a doctor?"

He laughs a pleasant laugh. "My mother likes to think I am."

I can't help but smile back at him, but it's an effort, because my whole body feels leaden and fuzzy.

"Are you in any pain?" he asks.

"I can't feel anything," I tell him, and that's when I notice that my right arm is wrapped in thick bandages and sitting on a pillow propped at a funny angle.

He nods. "Can you wiggle your fingers?"

I look at my hand and see something that looks like fingers sticking out from the bandages, but when I try to make them move, they just lie there.

"What's wrong with it?" I ask.

I'm expecting him to say that everything will be fine, but instead he shakes his head and says, "These wringer injuries are difficult. Your arm was badly hurt."

My mother moans as if it's her arm they're talking about.

"What's gonna happen to it?" I whisper.

"We'll just have to wait and see," he says.

"Tell me," I say. "You gotta tell me."

"Listen to the doctor, Penny," Me-me says,

trying to sound stern, but her voice is shaking. "We'll wait and see."

"Please," I beg.

Dr. Goldstein studies my face and says, "The nerves at your shoulder have been damaged." He pauses. "We hope they'll heal."

"What if they don't?" I ask.

"It's early yet," he says.

"What if they don't heal? What if they don't?" I demand, my voice rising.

"Then your arm may not work again," the doctor says gently. "I'm terribly sorry."

My mother starts crying, crying so hard that the nurse comes over and makes her sit down, and Me-me has her hand over her mouth, and there are tears running down her papery cheeks, and even Pop-pop, who always has something to say, opens his mouth but nothing comes out; he's like a fish gasping for air.

And me?

I close my eyes, and the whole world disappears.

CHAPTER SEVENTEEN

Dumb and Unlucky

Spending my summer vacation at the hospital is starting to be a bad habit. One of the nurses who was here last summer when I was in with my burned back remembered me.

"Try going to the beach next year," she suggested.

Ha-ha. A regular comedian.

I'm in the pediatric ward with the rest of the kids. Most of them can be divided into two categories: dumb or just plain unlucky.

The dumb kids include a boy who was baiting a dog and the dog decided he didn't like it and bit off half the kid's ear and took a good chunk out of one of his arms. Another knucklehead boy got burned by a camp stove when he was camping with the Boy Scouts, which just goes to show you that the Boy Scouts don't know as much as they're always saying. The dumbest boy is the one who's allergic to poison ivy but figured that burning it with some dried leaves in his backyard didn't count. His eyes are all swollen and he's covered from head to toe with oozing blisters. It's so bad that he even has blisters in his mouth. I've never seen anything like it. He looks like he should be in a monster movie. *The Poison Ivy Boy!*

The unlucky kid is a little girl who the nurses hover over. She has blood cancer, and the nurses whisper that she's *dying.*

And then there's me. Dumb *and* unlucky.

The hospital's just like a regular neighborhood, and after a while I know all the nurses and doctors, and even the orderlies. I prefer the nurses to the doctors; they spend time with you and talk to you and feed you and change your sheets and help you go to the bathroom, which, believe me, is pretty hard to do with just one arm when you can't leave the bed. I'm right-handed and now I can't do anything. It's the little things I miss most, like trying to brush my teeth or cut my own food, or even comb my stupid-looking hair. I never knew how important an arm was until now.

My Gregory Peck doctor is pretty nice, and our family doctor, Dr. Lathrop, checks on me every few days, but I don't like most of the other doctors. No wonder my mother quit being a nurse. A whole pack of doctors comes by every morning, and they wake me up and poke and prod me and talk about me like I'm not even there. They'll say, "The patient has reported that she has no sensation below the brachial plexus," and then they start talking all this medical mumbo jumbo. One morning I was so fed up that I interrupted them and said in a loud voice, "*The patient* has to go to the bathroom right now!" That got them out of here fast.

I get a lot of visitors. My mother comes by every morning, and when she leaves, Me-me and Pop-pop show up, and my father's family visits in the afternoons, and then my mother comes by again after work. I guess someone negotiated visiting times to avoid World War III.

My uncles give me presents, as usual. Uncle Nunzio brings me some fancy silk slippers with rabbit-fur trim and a matching silk robe. Uncle Ralphie brings me a box of pecan cookies, and Uncle Paulie gives me some Archie comic books, which I don't like very much, but they're better than nothing. All Betty and Veronica ever do is worry about dating stupid Archie and Reggie. My biggest present is a radio from Uncle Sally, so that

I won't miss any of the ball games. All the uncles visit, except for Uncle Dominic, who's the one I want to see most of all. Maybe he's scared to come to the hospital after what happened with my mother.

Frankie can come whenever he wants, even when visiting hours are over. The nurses think he's sweet because he gave them a big bunch of flowers. Red roses.

"Where'd you get them?" I ask him.

"Stole 'em from a dead lady upstairs," he tells me.

"You stole flowers from a dead lady?"

"It ain't like she needed them," he says, and eyes my arm. "Guess I'm gonna have to find a new shortstop."

"Frankie," I say.

"Sorry. Hey, it ain't all bad. We can get into ball games for free now!" He grins at me. "Wait'll the policemen get a look at your arm! You're better than that crippled kid!"

I just shake my head at him.

"What happened to all the money in Nonny's basement? Grandpa's treasure?"

Frankie's face falls. "Uncle Nunzio said it'll be used to pay for your hospital bill."

"It's gonna be some bill," I say.

It's not so bad, once you get past the boring part. I have a pretty busy schedule. Someone's always waking me to take my temperature or to change the bandages on my arm, or to put on clean sheets or feed me lunch, so by the end of the day I'm beat and I haven't done anything except lie in bed.

The other kids are okay—not that I can be choosy or anything. We're all in the same boat. Since I have a radio, I'm pretty popular. The nurses wheel the kids into a circle around my bed, and we sit and listen to the programs. They even let the girl with cancer get out of bed. They wheel her over but won't let the poison ivy kid sit near her.

We listen to *The Shadow* and *The Lone Ranger*. Somehow, hearing all the familiar voices makes things seem not so bad. We're like a regular family. We fight over what programs to listen to, and if someone talks, we tell him to be quiet.

When we're all laughing and shouting, I almost forget where I am.

"How are you feeling?" my mother asks when she arrives in the morning.

What she's really asking is if my arm is working, because Dr. Goldstein said if it doesn't move in the next few weeks, then it probably never will.

It'll just hang there for the rest of my life, like a roll of salami. But each day when I try to move my fingers, nothing happens. Some days I don't even think it's part of me.

"The same," I say. "I guess we won't be going to Lake George."

"No, we won't," she agrees. "I spoke with Aunt Francine, and she said that Lou Ellen was very upset when she heard you wouldn't be coming."

I'll just bet she was. She'll have to find someone else to torture.

She places a tin on my bedside table. "Me-me's oatmeal-raisin cookies. Maybe you can share them with the other kids."

"Mother, the other kids are trying to get better, not sicker."

She gives me a reluctant smile. Even though I'm the patient, I spend most of my time trying to make Mother feel better about things.

"Did you find the lucky bean?" I ask.

My mother nods and opens her handbag and then places the bean on the sheet.

"We tore the house apart looking for it," she says.

I pick it up with my good hand and give it a squeeze. I figure I need all the luck I can get now.

After my mother leaves, Me-me and Pop-pop

arrive. Me-me bustles about, straightening up my things, pouring me water, brushing my hair, while Pop-pop clomps around complaining about everything that's wrong with this place. He talks to anyone who will listen to him—the doctors, the nurses, you name it.

"I tell you what," he says loudly. "You should have your own room."

"They're for the really sick kids," I say.

"What? You're sick! Look at that arm of yours! Doesn't that count for anything? They want you to catch the plague?"

I sigh, and Pop-pop settles himself in the chair next to my bed. Next he'll start in on all the injured people he saw during the war.

"You know, when I was in Europe, I saw things that would make your insides turn purple," he says.

I yawn.

"There was this fella who had all his fingers blown right off. What do you think of that?"

The boy who got bit by the dog says, "Hey, if he didn't have any fingers, could he still pick his nose?"

Pop-pop scowls. "'Course he couldn't pick his nose. But he wasn't half as bad as this other fella, who got this fungus and his skin started to fall off."

The kid with the poison ivy pulls his sheet up higher.

"Enough with all that ghoulish talk," Me-me says to Pop-pop. "Go take a walk."

"What?" he says. "What?"

"I said, stop scaring Penny with all those awful stories," she says loudly.

"True stories is what they are," he grumbles, but he hobbles off with his cane.

"Here," Me-me says, placing a plate in front of me. "I brought you some meat loaf."

The hospital food is pretty awful, but Me-me's got it beat.

"The nurses'll be mad if I eat it," I lie, trying to look grave.

"I've never heard of such a thing," she says. "Turn away a nutritious meal?"

"They only want me eating what's on the trays. Doctors' orders."

She purses her lips and marches over to the nurses' station, and a few moments later she comes marching back with a satisfied expression on her face.

"Well, we don't have to worry about those pesky doctors' orders anymore," Me-me says, and beams. "That lovely nurse says you can eat whatever I bring you."

I groan before I can stop myself.

"Penny, dear, is your arm paining you?" Me-me asks.

"It sure is," I say.

Not to mention my stomach.

After lunch, Me-me and Pop-pop leave and my father's family starts showing up.

First is Uncle Paulie. He brings Aunt Gina and Nonny, who, of course, bursts into tears the minute she sees me.

"Hi, Nonny," I say.

"How ya doin', doll?" Aunt Gina asks.

"Still alive," I say.

"You look great," Uncle Paulie says, which is what he always says. "Don't she look great, Gina?"

Aunt Gina smiles at me. "I was thinking maybe we could go to New York City and see a show at Radio City when you get out of this joint."

"Really?" I ask.

She winks. "Sure, doll. I think you've earned a little fun."

Uncle Nunzio and Aunt Rosa show up next, and then come Uncle Sally and Uncle Ralphie. It's hard work being in the hospital. I never knew how much socializing was involved.

All my visitors want to know how I'm feeling, if the food's okay, if the bed's comfortable. Nobody will come right out and talk about my arm, even though it's hard to miss, kind of like Uncle Dominic living in the car.

Except Frankie, of course. He talks about my arm all the time.

"They gonna chop your arm off if it don't work?" he asks. "You know, amputate it?"

"How would I know?" I say. "They don't tell me anything."

"Why don't you ask the doctor?"

"Ask him yourself," I say.

Frankie goes right up to Dr. Goldstein. "Say, you gonna chop Penny's arm off if it don't get better?" he asks.

"Why do you want to know, young man?"

Frankie lowers his voice and says, "My uncle owns a butcher shop, and fresh arms get good money."

Dr. Goldstein grabs Frankie's arm and studies it. "In that case, I'm sure you'd be able to make some money on this specimen. I believe we have an operating room already prepared."

"Hey," Frankie says, yanking his arm back. "You even got a license?"

Dr. Goldstein winks at me, and I laugh.

After Frankie leaves, I have dinner, and then Mother stops by, and then it's lights-out. The nice nurse with the big laugh, Miss Simkins, comes over and makes sure we're okay. All the kids on the ward like her better than Miss Lombardo, who's kind of stern.

This is the rottenest part of the day. When the ward is bright and sunny and the nurses are rushing about and visitors are coming and going, it's easy to be brave, to believe that everything's going to be okay after all. It's harder at night, when the ward is dark and quiet. I miss home. I miss Mother's voice and Pop-pop's burping, and I sort of miss Me-me's cooking. I even miss the toilet leaking on my bed.

"You still awake, Penny?" the boy in the bed next to me whispers. He's the one who got bit by the dog. His name is Jonathan.

"Yeah," I say. "My back itches and I can't scratch it."

"I hate it here," he says. "Food's terrible."

"You haven't eaten at my house," I say.

"I hate it here too," another kid whispers farther down.

"Me too!" says another.

Pretty soon we're all complaining about the place, like we have any say in it at all. Maybe we can start a club: the Dumb and Unlucky Kids.

I lie there and think of all the things I may never get to do. I'll never be able to drive a car or put both my arms around Jack Teitelzweig's back while he whispers in my ear that I'm the most beautiful girl in the room, which I won't be. I'll be the girl that mothers point out to their children, the dumb one who doesn't have any sense. Like a character from one of Frankie's comics.

The One-Armed Girl.

"I'm sorry, Penny," my movie-star doctor says. "But there's no avoiding it."

The doctors had been waiting to see if the skin under my armpit would get better. But it got ground up pretty good by the wringer, and now they say I have to have a skin graft, which means an operation. The doctors are gonna borrow some skin from my thigh and put it under my arm. It sounds terrible to me. Mother's not very happy about this either, but Frankie's eyes practically bug out when I tell him.

"Holy Toledo!" he says. "They're gonna carve skin off you and sew it under your arm?"

"That's what they're saying," I say.

"You're gonna look like Frankenstein!"

"Thanks a lot, Frankie," I say.

"Nah, it's great!" he says. "Now I just gotta get a camera."

"What for?"

He looks at me like I'm stupid. "So I can take pictures, of course! People pay to see gruesome things like that!"

The next morning when they come to take me in for the operation, I'm feeling pretty scared. What if I end up like Cora Lamb, in the cemetery being visited by her mother? What if I die? What then?

Mother kisses me on the forehead.

"I love you, Bunny," she says.

"I'll take good care of her, Eleanor," Dr. Goldstein tells my mother as they wheel me out.

The operating room is a buzz of activity. I look up and see my movie-star doctor staring down at me on the table.

"Did you know that your mother and I started at the hospital at the same time, Penny?" Dr. Goldstein asks.

"Mother told me," I say. "Did you know my father?"

He hesitates and then says, "No. But your mother was my favorite nurse." He winks. "Didn't listen to a thing I said, but she always laughed at my jokes."

"Tell me one," I say.

"How do you stop a nose from running?" Dr. Goldstein asks.

"I don't know. How?"

"Trip it," he says, and grins.

I manage a smile. "You're better than Pop-pop."

"I'll tell you another one when you wake up."

Then a different doctor holds a mask over my nose and says, "Now take deep breaths."

The last thing I hear is Frankie's voice and one of the doctors saying: "I don't care if you're the president of the United States, kid. No pictures allowed. Now scram!"

CHAPTER EIGHTEEN

The Last Person on Earth

I decide that when it comes right down to it, people like a good tragedy.

Like my father dying. One day he was writing for the newspaper, eating my mother's roast chicken, and the next day he was sick. He died, they buried him, and everyone was real sad.

But me they don't know what to do with anymore. The operation was successful, but my arm still doesn't work. My visitors always seem confused about how to act. It's pretty clear I'm not going to die, but they don't know how upset to be. After all, you can't hold a funeral for a dead arm or visit it in Shady Grove Cemetery.

All the kids who were here when I came in are gone, except the cancer girl, who's hanging on longer than anyone thought. We hear about a new boy on the isolation ward who's got polio. The nurses talk about him, how he's in an iron lung. They're even saying that his mother thinks he got it from the pool.

When Frankie comes by to visit, we play gin rummy.

I'm feeling cranky. I'm sick of this place. But that isn't the only thing that's bothering me. I keep expecting Uncle Dominic to show up, but he doesn't. He hasn't visited me once the whole time I've been in here. Even some of the girls from school who don't talk to me sent a card.

"Stop losing on purpose," I say after I win the fourth game in a row.

"What?" Frankie says with an innocent look.

"Why won't Uncle Dominic visit me?" I ask. "Is he all right?"

"I dunno."

"Frankie," I say.

He holds up his hands. "I don't. Nobody knows where he is. He's disappeared. Took his car and nobody's seen him since the day you got hurt."

"You gotta find out where he went," I say.

The next morning when Frankie comes in, he's wearing a triumphant smile.

"I got the goods, all right," he announces.

"Well?" I demand.

"He's in Florida," he says.

"Florida?"

"I think he's a ruthless killer now," Frankie says.

"What are you talking about?" I ask.

He lowers his voice. "It explains everything. You know, why he lives in his car and all that. Killers can't have a permanent address."

"Where'd you hear that?"

"Around."

"Frankie, you gotta stop reading those crime comics," I tell him.

He leaves, and I lie in bed holding the lucky bean in my one good hand, trying to picture Uncle Dominic standing on the beach in Florida, staring out at the ocean. No matter how I look at it, I just don't understand.

How can one of the most important people in your life disappear like he was never really there?

I watch my mother talking to the doctors in the hallway.

My Gregory Peck doctor says something and her shoulders slump. She doesn't say a word when she comes over to my bed, but I see it in her eyes. It looks like she's trying to hold back tears. That's when I know it's all over, that my arm is never gonna work.

Just like that.

"You can have my bike," I tell Frankie when he comes by later that day.

"I can?" he asks, excited. But then he realizes that this doesn't make much sense. He looks at me suspiciously.

"Nah," he says. "What'd I want a girls' bike for, anyway? You'll be riding it in no time, you watch."

I look away from him, out the window.

"Come on," he says, picking up the pudding from my lunch tray and starting in on it. "Knock it off with the sour puss."

Frankie eats the rest of my lunch and tries to get me to laugh at some stupid joke he heard, but I don't, and finally he gives up and leaves.

"You feeling okay, hon?" Miss Simkins asks, putting her hand on my forehead.

"Can I have a pain pill, please?"

"Sure, sweetheart," she says. "I'll be right back."

When the fuzzy feeling hits my blood, I close my eyes and block out the sounds of the ward. I imagine I'm someone else, some other girl who has a regular life, who has two working arms.

The girl I used to be.

They move the cancer girl's bed next to mine so she can have a friend. Which is just what I need, seeing as how she's going to die any day now.

She's only eight, and her name is Gwendolyn, but she says to call her Gwennie. Gwennie has this sad-looking nearly bald doll that she calls Annabelle and keeps in bed with her.

"You sure got a lot of family," Gwennie says after a pack of the uncles leaves one afternoon. She just has a mother and father who visit her.

"Yeah."

"You Italian?" she asks.

"Half," I say.

"I like pizza," she says. "But my mother says we can only have it as a treat."

After that, I give her all the food that the relatives bring, and for a girl who's dying, she sure has a healthy appetite.

"When you get out of here, you should go over to my Nonny's house. She'd love you," I tell her.

"How come?"

"You're a good eater," I say.

"I'm not getting out," Gwennie says.

I don't say anything to that.

"Your arm," she asks. "Is it gonna work again?"

And what's the point of lying?

"No," I say.

She dies two days later.

I send back my meal trays untouched. The nurse says something to my mother.

"Bunny," my mother says, "you have to eat something."

"I'm not hungry," I say.

It seems like everyone and their uncle starts showing up with food. Me-me brings a tuna casserole, Mother brings roast chicken, and Frankie stops by with a bag of fresh doughnuts. Aunt Gina brings macaroni, Uncle Ralphie brings candy from the store, Uncle Paulie brings filet mignon, and Uncle Sally brings a box of *sfogliatelle*, but I don't touch any of it. I just can't.

Nonny appears in the doorway the next day, right before dinner. She's wearing a black dress and carrying a plate of *pastiera*. She sits in the chair next to my bed, looking like a black angel against all the white of the hospital.

"Tesoro mio," she says, "eat."

Something in her voice makes me open my mouth, and before I have a chance to shut it, she pops a piece of *pastiera* in like I'm a baby, and it tastes so good, like it's the best thing I've ever eaten in my whole life. She feeds me another piece, and I keep waiting for her to burst into tears, but she just looks at me, her eyes so sad, and I don't know what it is, but the tears start rolling down my cheeks, and once I start I can't seem to stop. And pretty soon I'm crying for everything—for my arm, for Scarlett O'Hara, for Gwennie, for Uncle Dominic, for my poor dead father, for the great big mess my life has become. I bawl so hard, you'd think rivers would flood and houses would float away.

I cry and cry and cry, and Nonny just holds me tight, her two strong arms the only thing keeping me from drowning in it all.

I'm staring out the window.

"Penny," Miss Simkins says to me, "you have a visitor."

Mr. Mulligan is standing in the doorway, a newspaper tucked under one arm and a paper bag in the other. He's the last person on earth I expected to see here, especially after how I've behaved.

He doesn't seem to think anything's unusual,

because he just drags up a chair beside my bed and pulls out a container of ice cream from the paper bag.

"I heard you like butter pecan," he says.

"I'll get some bowls and spoons," Miss Simkins says with a smile.

Mr. Mulligan's not like any of my other visitors. He doesn't want to know how I feel or whether I've tried my arm that day. He doesn't ask if I need something to drink or eat. He just unfolds the newspaper and starts reading to me out loud from the sports section. His voice is deep and lulling.

"The Brooklyn Dodgers . . ."

I close my eyes and listen.

Mr. Mulligan comes every day after his milk deliveries and reads me the paper cover to cover.

We start with the sports section and then go on to local news and then to the obituaries, which are more interesting than you would think. After this we move on to the funnies section. Mr. Mulligan uses all sorts of silly voices to act out the characters. He does a great Blondie and Dagwood. Our favorite section is the police blotter. In the last week alone, there's been one bicycle theft and a missing pet, and Mrs. Agnes Sloff reported seeing an "unusual" man peeping in her front window. We both agree that the police chief sure has his work cut out for him keeping up with the local criminals.

Mr. Mulligan's an interesting fella. Before becoming a milkman, he was in the air force and was stationed in Burma during the war. He says the worst part was after the war was over.

"Took us nearly a year to get home," he says.

"A whole year?" I ask.

"And we didn't even get a plane ride back. Can you believe that? We had to take a ship, and it took thirty-three days. The Japanese had put all these floating mines in the ocean to blow up the American ships, but we had to go right through them to get back home."

"What'd you do?" I say.

"There were minesweepers. They'd clear the mines so the ships could get through."

"Sounds dangerous," I say.

"One time I was sleeping belowdecks, and I guess the captain thought that we'd cleared the mines, and I heard all this shouting. I ran up on deck to see what was going on. Turns out the minesweepers missed one, and this mine was floating right toward us!"

"Really? Right at you?"

He nods. "All the boys on deck were shooting at it, but they were so nervous and shook up that they kept missing it."

"What happened?"

"Well, this marine came running up with his gun and stood there, calm as can be, and took one shot and *bam!* He got it."

"Holy moly!" I say.

"Just goes to show you that you should always keep a marine around," he says, and chuckles.

"I'll remember that," I say.

I look at Mr. Mulligan with his balding head and kind eyes.

"I'm glad there was a marine on your ship," I tell him.

"Me too," he says, and smiles.

CHAPTER NINETEEN

The Bomb

It's late. My eyes are closed and I'm trying to sleep, but I can't.

School's started, and I never thought I'd say it, but I miss school. I miss the hallways and the teachers and the homework and even mean old Veronica Goodman. I would give my right arm to be back in school, ha-ha.

Everything is dark except for the light at the nurses' station. Most nights the orderlies and nurses sit around playing cards and talking. One of the orderlies, a fella named Harvey, is flirting with Miss Simkins. Their soft voices drift over to me.

"Why you wasting time with that doctor?" Harvey asks.

Miss Simkins laughs. "Who says I'm wasting time?"

"C'mon," Harvey says. "Now, me? I'd treat you real good."

"Yeah?" she says.

"Yeah," he says. "So how 'bout it?"

She doesn't say anything.

"How's the girl with the arm doing?" Harvey asks.

Miss Simkins makes a *tsk*ing sound.

"Poor kid," he says. "Jimmy told me her father was the one who had all the trouble. You know her mother then?"

"Before my time. Sheila was here, though."

"So he was really a spy?"

I feel like I've been punched in the stomach so hard that I don't know if I'll ever get my breath back.

"Must've been," she says. "They took him away, didn't they?"

"Never can tell. What happened to him, any-how?"

"Died in jail, I heard . . . ," she says, and then she lowers her voice and I can't hear her any-more.

I stare into the dark, and for some reason all I can think about is Pop-pop's friend the translator. Now I know why he isn't smiling in the photo-graph. It's because even though he got answers to his questions, he knew nothing would ever be the same after that bomb was dropped.

Which is what just happened to me here.

Mother doesn't come first thing in the morning because she has errands to run. I have to wait until lunchtime. But for once I don't care about upsetting her. I need to know.

"Hi, Bunny," my mother says. "I brought you some pecan cookies."

"I know about my father being a spy," I blurt out. "You lied to me!"

The blood drains from her face. Then she covers her mouth with her hand, her eyes welling with tears.

"Mother?"

But instead of answering, she just turns and runs out of the room, right past Aunt Gina and Uncle Paulie, who are coming in.

"Was that your mother?" Aunt Gina asks.

"Was my father a spy?" I demand.

Uncle Paulie pales.

"He was, wasn't he? Why won't anyone ever tell me anything?" I ask, my voice rising.

He looks helplessly at Aunt Gina.

"Paulie, go see if Ellie's okay, why don't ya?" she snaps, and a moment later he is gone.

"You gotta tell me," I plead.

"He wasn't a spy," Aunt Gina says, and sits in the chair beside my bed. She pulls a pack of cigarettes out of her handbag and taps one out, her hand trembling. Then she lights it and takes a long drag and blows it out slowly.

"It all started with the radio," she says in a dull voice.

"What radio?"

She doesn't answer. Finally she says, "Your father loved going to ball games. But after you were born, he didn't want to spend a minute away from you, so Dominic went out and bought this fancy brand-new radio so your father could listen to the games at home. One night your folks were sitting down to dinner, the doorbell rang, and some FBI agents came and took your father away. Took them both away, I should say."

"Both?"

"When the FBI came to see Dominic about the radio, he said that your father had it, so they dragged both of them in for questioning."

"Because of a radio?" I ask, bewildered.

"Italians weren't allowed to have this kind of radio. See, after Pearl Harbor, the whole country went crazy. All of a sudden everyone was suspicious of foreigners. They passed this law: If you were Italian and didn't have your citizenship, you couldn't travel to certain places, or have radios with a shortwave band, or flashlights, or cameras, or I don't know what else."

"But what's this got to do with my father?" I ask.

"Your father was born in Italy and came over when he was two. But it turned out that Grandfather Falucci never finished the paperwork, so your father and Nonny weren't citizens. Freddy had begun applying for citizenship, but then the war started. So he and Nonny had to go and register as 'enemy aliens.' They had their photographs taken, got fingerprinted, the whole works."

"Nonny?" I gasp. "They fingerprinted my Nonny? What was she gonna do? Feed someone to death?"

Aunt Gina throws her hands up in exasperation. "They thought that the Italians might be spies. They didn't even want you speaking Italian."

It's all so much to take in that my head is spinning.

"The FBI wouldn't listen when Freddy tried to explain that it was all a misunderstanding. Especially when they found out about him being an 'enemy alien' and writing for that Italian-language newspaper. And he didn't even write about politics for that Italian paper," she says in frustration. "He wrote for the society section. He wrote about parties! Picnics!"

"What happened?"

"They let Dominic go, but they took Freddy to Ellis Island, and then he was sent to this army base in Maryland. They put him in an internment camp there. Your mother visited him, and we kept thinking they'd realize they'd made a mistake and let him come home," she says, and swallows. "Nobody saw him after he was sent to another internment camp in Oklahoma."

"Is that where he died?" I whisper.

"Yeah, he died in that camp. Near about killed your mother when she heard. Your uncle, too. Dominic ain't been right since."

"Is that why he quit playing ball?"

Aunt Gina nods.

"So my father wasn't a spy?" I say.

"Doll," she says sadly, "his only crime was being Italian."

Then she looks past me at Uncle Paulie walking toward us with Mother. My mother's eyes are raw with grief, and Uncle Paulie doesn't look too good either.

"Aunt Gina told me everything," I say when they reach us.

Mother nods, her lips tight, but she sits down.

"C'mon, Paulie," Aunt Gina says, and tugs the curtain around us for privacy.

Then it's just me and my mother.

"I never wanted you to hear that," she says, and her voice breaks. "Never. Your father was a good man. He loved this country."

"How did he die?"

My mother's eyes are shiny when she looks at me. "They said he had a gastric hemorrhage. He must have been sick for a while. I still can't bear to think of him dying alone, far from all of us." She takes a deep breath.

"The way people looked at us when they found out. Here at the hospital my supervisor made a snide comment, and after that, I quit. I just couldn't work with people who would say such things." She shakes her head. "When your father died, I didn't think I'd be able to go on. I was so angry. At everything. We had a perfect life and it was ruined. For nothing! For a radio!"

I think of my father dying all alone, and the tears start running down my face. "But why did Uncle Dominic buy the radio? I thought he loved my father! How could he do that?"

Something in her face softens. "Believe me, I know it's easy to blame Dominic. But it wasn't his fault, not really. Dominic didn't think he had anything to worry about when he bought that radio; he was a citizen. He just walked in and asked them for the best radio they had. He wasn't thinking of what could happen. We were all so young." My mother sighs and looks away. "I've been angry for so long, and just when I started to feel better, this happened." She winces. "It wasn't fair of me to yell at Dominic like that, though. It all sort of caught up with me."

"I wish you'd told me all this before," I say.

"It was just too hard. How could we have explained it to you? It seemed easier to keep it a secret. And we didn't want you to be ashamed. That was the *one* thing we all agreed upon."

"Can I ask you something?"

She nods.

And then I ask the question I've always wanted to ask: "What did my father think of me?"

"Oh, Bunny, he loved you so much," my mother says with a gentle smile. "He called you *cocca di papà*. 'Daddy's little girl.'"

My heart goes still.

We sit there for a moment, the noises of the hospital washing over us.

"Mother," I say.

"Yes?"

"Can I ask you one more question?"

"Ask anything you want," she says, and her voice grows stronger. "Anything at all. I promise, no more secrets."

"Will you please scratch my back? It's really itchy."

They move a new kid into the bed next to mine, another girl.

Her name's Vivian and she just got her appendix out; she's not dying or anything serious like that. She has an older brother who gives her this magazine with comics called *Tales Calculated to Drive You MAD*, which is awfully funny.

We whisper to each other after lights-out, and Mr. Mulligan brings ice cream for both of us. It's nice to have a new friend.

"He sure is swell," Vivian tells me after Mr. Mulligan leaves.

"I know. You feeling any better?" I ask.

"I'm sore," she says, and grimaces. "I wish I had my lucky rabbit's foot. I know I'd get better faster if I had that."

"You can borrow my lucky bean," I say.

"What's a lucky bean?" she asks, curious.

I nod toward it. It's sitting on my bedside table.

"It's for good luck," I tell her. "My uncle Dominic gave it to me."

"The one who lives in the car?"

"Yeah, that one."

"Can I see it?" she asks.

I lean over for it, but because I'm balanced kind of oddly, I knock the table and the lucky bean starts to slide off. I don't think; I just reach for it with my bad arm.

I reach.

My arm moves, my fingers curl, and just like that, I have my life back.

CHAPTER TWENTY

What's in a Name

It's a miracle, but not like the miracles you hear about in church.

My arm doesn't start working all perfectly. At first it's only my fingers, but soon my hand is moving. It's the middle of September when they let me go home. I have to wear bandages and a sling and promise to do exercises, but at this point I'd promise to eat Me-me's liver seven nights a week just to get out of the hospital.

I go home to find that my bedroom has been completely redecorated.

"Do you like it?" Me-me asks, her hands folded in front of her.

The poodles are gone, and the walls have been painted a pale turquoise, the color of the ocean.

There's a white chenille bedspread and new lamps with fancy glass bases. It looks sort of like Aunt Gina's bedroom.

"And how!" I say.

"He missed a spot," Pop-pop says, pointing at the wall with his cane.

"Don't start with that again," Me-me tells him.

"Who missed a spot?" I ask.

"That Mulligan fella painted the room," Pop-pop grumbles. "Your mother and grandmother didn't want me going up on the ladder. I told 'em I could do it, but they ganged up on me."

I raise my eyebrows but don't say anything.

My arm gets stronger by the day, and when I go to see Dr. Goldstein, he's impressed with the progress I'm making.

"You're going to end up in the textbooks," he says.

"As long as I don't end up back in the hospital," I say. "No offense."

"None taken," Dr. Goldstein says.

"You know," I say, "you kinda look like Gregory Peck."

"I hear that a lot," he says, and flashes me a smile good as any movie star's.

Aunt Gina takes me to a fancy hair salon, and Uncle Nunzio has a bunch of new dresses made for me. Between the haircut and the dresses, I look glamorous, like a new girl.

I start going back to school. Suddenly I'm real popular. Boys offer to carry my books. It seems that almost dying is a good way to improve your social life. Even Veronica Goodman leaves me alone, which is nearly as good as my arm working.

Everyone asks the same question: "How much did it hurt?"

"A lot," I always say, and watch their eyes go round with awe and something else—admiration. I want to tell them that almost dying is awfully easy.

It's the living that's hard.

One afternoon after school Pop-pop brings me a brown box. I can hear something inside, scratching to be let out. I open the box, and a little black kitten with a smudge of white fur on its side scrambles out.

"Figured you could use some company," Pop-pop says, clearing his throat.

"She's so sweet!" I say, rubbing my face in the kitten's fur.

He scowls. "She? She? It's a boy! Don't they teach you anything in that school of yours?"

I laugh.

"What're you going to call him?" he asks.

"I don't know," I say.

"Cat needs a name. Everybody needs a name."

I look seriously at the kitten. The kitten looks back at me. And I know right away what to name him.

"Well?" Pop-pop asks.

"I'm going to call him Rhett."

"What?" he asks. "What did you say?"

"I said, 'I'm going to call him Rhett,'" I say loudly. "You know, like Rhett Butler. *Gone with the Wind*?"

"Rhett, eh? Could do worse, I reckon, although not much," he says.

"Thanks, Pop-pop."

"You're my granddaughter," he says gruffly.

"I love you," I say, and hug him.

For once, he hears me just fine.

Everything's different now. Better somehow. Mr. Mulligan comes over for dinner all the time, and he fixes the toilet when it leaks.

Frankie's still working at the factory, and he loves Uncle Nunzio. That's all he talks about: How smart Uncle Nunzio is; how he wants to be a businessman just like Uncle Nunzio when he grows up; how Uncle Nunzio has promised to help him with college if he stays out of trouble.

"I only got one more month, and then that window is all paid up," Frankie says proudly. "Uncle Nunzio says I'm one of the best workers he ever had."

"That's swell," I say.

A crafty look comes over his face. "Listen. I have a hunch Grandpa buried money all over that house. If we can just get back in—"

"Frankie . . ."

"We'll be rich!"

I look at him and shake my arm.

"Yeah," he says finally. "Who needs money, anyhow? We got everything we need, right?"

"Right," I say.

"But you know how many ball games we could see with all that money?" Frankie wheedles. "We could *buy* the Dodgers with that kind of money!"

I sigh.

A new movie opens at the theater and I ask my mother if I can go see it.

"You want to end up in an iron lung?" she says.

I guess some things don't change after all.

Two more miracles happen that are almost as good as my arm working again. The first happens real quiet-like.

I'm still working at Falucci's, but only after school. Since I can't do any real work around the store, Aunt Fulvia has me be the one to sit up front and work the register. Uncle Ralphie hires another kid to help with the deliveries. It's Eugene Bird.

"Boy looks quiet, but he always gets paid," Aunt Fulvia tells me approvingly.

I'm sitting at the register doing my homework when the bell on the door rings. I look up and see Jack Teitelzweig standing there. He smiles, a big honest-to-goodness smile, and I feel a tickle in my stomach.

"How are you doing, Penny?" he asks.

"Uh—um, good," I stammer.

He turns serious. "How's your arm? Does it still hurt?"

I nod. "Some."

"I like your haircut," he says, and I blush.

"Jack Teitelzweig!" Uncle Ralphie calls in his booming voice, coming up front. "How are you, Jack?"

"Very well, Mr. Falucci," Jack says.

Aunt Fulvia pokes her head out from the back to see what's going on.

Uncle Ralphie looks confused. "Did your mother call in an order?"

"Actually, I'm here to see Penny," he says, and swallows.

"I see." Uncle Ralphie looks between me and Jack. "Well, I better get back and help your aunt. Call me if you need anything."

Uncle Ralphie goes into the back, and I hear my Aunt Fulvia demand in a loud voice, "Ralphie, who is that boy out there talking to our Penny?"

"It's Jack Teitelzweig."

"Teitelzweig?" Aunt Fulvia says. "That's not an Italian name."

"He's a nice boy, *patanella mia*," Uncle Ralphie whispers fiercely.

I wince.

"What does *patanella mia* mean?" Jack asks, curious.

"'My little potato,'" I say, my cheeks burning.

"You should hear what my mother calls my father," he says, and I laugh.

We stare at each other for a moment.

Then Jack Teitelzweig says to me, Penny Falucci, "Would you like to go see a movie with me sometime?"

"My mother won't let me go to the movie theater," I say automatically. "She's afraid I'll catch polio."

"Oh," he says, and his face falls. "We could

always go for ice cream. Do you like ice cream?"

"I love ice cream," I say. "Butter pecan is my favorite."

"Mine too," he says, and grins at me.

That's the exact moment I know I'm in love.

The second miracle happens real loud and makes all the newspapers. The Dodgers are in the World Series against the New York Yankees. Finally, a chance for revenge after last year's defeat!

Even though Dem Bums are in the Series, I'm feeling a little blue. The one person who would be as excited as me about the Dodgers isn't here.

The Bronx Bombers win the first two games, but Dem Bums come back and win the next two and we're tied. Things start to change around game five. That's when Mr. Mulligan shows up with the television set. Mr. Mulligan still talks too much through the game, but even Frankie agrees that he's not so bad.

"Think he could get me a deal on a television set?" Frankie asks.

We're so excited to be watching the game on television that we almost forgive the Dodgers for losing game five.

Game six is at Yankee Stadium. We're biting

our nails up to the ninth inning, trailing the Yankees, when a miracle happens. Our man Carl Furillo sends a two-run homer into the right-field stands, tying the game three all! The Dodgers fans in the stadium go crazy, and so do we!

"Did you see that?" I say, jumping up and down. "We're tied! We're tied!"

"It's not over yet," Mr. Mulligan says. "The Yanks are up at bat, and they've got that young Billy Martin."

We all hold our breath. The Yanks have one man on base when Billy Martin takes the plate. There's the pitch and—*whammo!* Billy Martin hits a hard drive to center field, bringing a man home. It's all over.

"Those lousy Bums," Frankie says sourly.

When the Dodgers lose the World Series again, hearts break all over Brooklyn.

And a few hearts break in New Jersey, too.

It's a quiet Saturday morning, and I'm sitting on the summer porch watching Rhett run back and forth, chasing squirrels in the backyard. It's so funny, almost like Scarlett O'Hara has told him to keep the squirrels out.

"Hi, Princess," a voice says.

I look up to see Uncle Dominic standing there. He's thin, thinner than ever, and there are dark circles under his eyes, but he's tan.

"Florida?" I say.

"Yeah," he says, and tries to smile, but his mouth is strained. He sits carefully on the chair across from me. "How's your arm?"

But I'm mad at him. Mad at him for abandoning me when I needed him, and mad at him for what happened to my father, too.

"Hurts a lot," I say.

His eyes are haunted. "Princess," he says.

"Mother told me what happened to my father. She told me everything," I say.

He flinches. "She did?"

I nod.

He starts talking, talking so fast I can barely understand him.

"She's right, you know. It was all my fault," he says, the words spilling out of him in a rush. "My big mouth. I was always bragging, bragging to everyone. I told the whole world when I bought that radio for Freddy. These neighbors of ours, the Clarkes, they never liked us very much. Didn't like Italians. They had to be the ones who called the Feds. When those men came looking for that radio, I told them I gave it to Freddy. I told them!"

He's shaking now. "They took us in, and I kept telling him, 'Freddy, it's all a mistake, we'll be home by dinnertime, you watch.' And then they let me go but not him! Not him!" His eyes stare past me in horror, like he's trapped in a nightmare and can't wake up.

And that's when I realize how wrong I am about being mad at him. He's my uncle Dominic, the uncle who would do anything for me.

"Uncle Dominic," I say, "it wasn't your fault."

"You know why you're called Penny?" he asks with a sad smile.

"Because of the song. 'Pennies from Heaven.' It was my father's favorite song."

He makes a small choked sound, something between a laugh and a sob. "We didn't start calling you Penny until after your father died. You were always Barbara before then."

"Uncle Dominic—"

"Freddy wrote us when he was in that last camp. He was sick. He knew he was dying, and all he could think about was you. He wrote, 'That baby's just like a lost penny I'll never hold again,'" Uncle Dominic says, his voice breaking. "*My lost penny.*'"

I shake my head wordlessly.

"I killed my own brother!" He buries his face

in his hands and starts sobbing, a horrible noise, like his very heart is being ripped out, and all I know is that it feels like mine is being ripped out too.

"Oh, Uncle Dominic," I say, and it's my turn finally to give him something, something he won't give himself: forgiveness. "You're wrong."

He looks up.

"My father called me Penny because he loved Bing Crosby."

"No, he didn't, he—"

I reach over and grab his hand and hold it tight. "He did. He said, 'Let's call the baby Penny because she's going to be shiny and bright. She's going to be as wonderful as my brother Dominic.'"

And maybe it's because it's me saying it, but his face changes and his tears stop.

"You know what else?" I say. "If I hadn't had the lucky bean, I bet my arm would never have worked again. Why, my fingers started working when I reached for it! I know it was the bean."

"You really think so?" he asks skeptically.

"The doctors say it was a miracle," I say in an earnest voice.

He looks like he's going to buy it, and I exhale a sigh of relief.

Then he narrows his eyes and asks, "Who taught you to lie so good?"

I make a face. "Frankie."

He shakes his head and holds up a finger. "No more digging up basements."

"No more basements," I promise.

"That's more like it," he says.

We sit there for a moment.

"What were you doing in Florida, anyhow?" I ask him.

"Why?"

"Frankie's been telling everyone that you're a ruthless killer."

"Me?" He laughs.

"Yeah," I say. "Are you?"

"Not unless you count fish," he says.

"Fish?" I say.

Uncle Dominic tugs his wallet out of his pocket and pulls out a photograph of him standing next to a marlin.

"Frankie's gonna be disappointed," I say.

"Tell him to get in line," he says.

"I can't believe Dem Bums lost the World Series," I say wistfully. "They should've won."

"They will someday, you watch. You gotta have faith."

"I wish you'd been here," I say in a quiet voice.

"The whole time I was listening to it, I was thinking of you," Uncle Dominic says.

"You were?"

"Always, Princess," he says, and I know it's the truth. "Always."

CHAPTER TWENTY-ONE

A Lucky Girl

Mr. Mulligan shows up on our porch after school. He's wearing a suit and tie, not his milkman uniform, and has a paper bag in one hand.

"You get the afternoon off?" I ask when I open the door.

"Something like that," he says, and he fiddles with his tie nervously.

"Mother's at work," I tell him.

"Actually," he says, "I wanted to talk to you. May I come in?"

"Sure," I say, wondering why he's acting so funny. We walk into the parlor, and he sits on the love seat and I sit on the padded chair.

"Who's that?" Me-me calls from the kitchen.

"Mr. Mulligan," I call back.

"Oh," she says in a pleased voice. "Why don't I bring lemonade in for you two?"

Me-me comes in with a tray of lemonade and oatmeal cookies and sets it out before us.

"Those cookies are fresh from the oven. Now, you two have a nice visit," she announces before bustling off.

We sit there in silence for a moment. Mr. Mulligan reaches for a cookie.

"I wouldn't if I were you," I say, and he puts it back.

"Uh, Penny," Mr. Mulligan says, clearing his throat loudly. "I, ahem, I was wondering if you would give me your permission to marry your mother."

I look around. Me?

"Shouldn't you be asking Pop-pop?" I say.

"Your mother said I should ask you first," he says.

"Oh," I say.

"Gee, I love your mother an awful lot," he says, his leg bouncing.

I don't say anything.

"I promise I'll be real good to her, and to you, of course," he says quickly, wiping away a drop of sweat. "And Pop-pop and Me-me."

I swing my legs.

"I know I can't replace your father, but I'll do my best to be a good dad," he says.

We sit there a moment longer.

He swallows hard. "Well, what do you say?"

"What's in the bag?" I ask.

"Ice cream," he says.

"What flavor?"

"Butter pecan," he says with a slow grin.

What can I say to an offer like that?

My mother wears a peach dress and carries a spray of stephanotis, and Mr. Mulligan wears a dark suit. I get to be the flower girl and maid of honor all in one. Instead of me carrying a bouquet, Frankie has the bright idea of twining flowers all around my sling, which looks sort of fancy, or sort of like something Tarzan would do, depending on how you look at it. Either way, the judge compliments me on my arm. Afterward we all have lunch at a fancy hotel, and my mother's smiling like she's the luckiest girl in the world.

Mr. Mulligan says I can call him whatever I want, so I tell him I want to call him Pat, which he thinks is just fine. Maybe someday I'll call him Dad, but not yet. We have plenty of time. He's not going anywhere.

When Pat moved into the house, I was kind of

worried. After all, Pop-pop's not real good at compromise, and he likes to give a lot of advice. But for some reason Pat seems to know how to handle him without being driven crazy. Whenever Pop-pop tells him to do this or that, Pat just smiles and says, "Hmm, I'll have to give that some thought."

Pat does things a little different. He's spontaneous. He thinks nothing of waking me up after I've gone to bed at night to surprise me with a pizza or hand-dipped ice cream. He likes to stay up late playing charades and poker. And his favorite thing is to go to Howard Johnson's for dinner and order pancakes. Now on Friday nights instead of staying home with me and Me-me and Pop-pop, my mother puts on the fox stole and goes out dancing with Pat. It's hard getting used to having someone new in the house, but it's like Me-me always says: It's nice to have a man around who knows how to fix the toilet.

One night after dinner, I'm helping my mother dry dishes while Me-me washes them.

Lately she's been talking about going back to nursing. Dr. Lathrop is looking for a nurse for his practice.

"Might be nice," she says. "Regular hours and all. No hospital."

I know better than to say anything, and for once, Me-me does too.

"Pop-pop said he saw your Uncle Dominic yesterday," Mother says in a careful voice.

"He was in Florida," I say. "Fishing."

She allows herself a small smile. "He always did like to fish. Your father, too. I think his grandfather, your great-grandfather, was a fisherman back in Italy."

I can't believe my mother's talking about my father's family like this.

"Why don't you get along with them?" I ask, trying to sound casual.

Mother looks surprised for a second, but then she says, "I know you love them, but they were a hard family to marry into. They're kind of overwhelming, especially your grandmother."

"Nonny?"

"She terrified me. We weren't married a week when she announced she was moving in with us to help take care of things."

"What happened?" I ask.

My mother chuckles. "You would have thought the world had ended when your father told her no!

You have to understand, none of them were very happy about our marriage, except Dominic. They had an Italian girl all picked out for your father. After he died, things were difficult. I don't think your grandmother Falucci will ever forgive me for Freddy not being buried in the Catholic cemetery." She takes a breath. "I agreed to let you get to know them, but we all just kept our distance from each other."

I dry a plate and put it on the stack.

My mother turns to me. "Why don't you see if they want to come over for dinner?"

"Really?"

"Sure," she says, and lowers her voice. "If we can survive Me-me's liver, we can survive anything."

Everyone comes. Nonny, Uncle Paulie and Aunt Gina, Uncle Nunzio and Aunt Rosa, Uncle Ralphie and Aunt Fulvia, Uncle Angelo and Aunt Teresa, Uncle Sally, and Frankie and the baby cousins, too. There's so many of them, like their own ball club or something.

My mother has taken extra care with her hair and is wearing a new dress.

Nonny walks right up the steps to my mother.

"Eleanor," she says.

"Genevieve," my mother says, and I'm so shocked I can barely breathe. I didn't even know my grandmother had a first name!

"Your hair," Nonny says. "You cut."

"Yes," my mother replies in an even voice. "Yes, I did."

My grandmother looks at her for a long minute and then nods in approval.

We go into the parlor, and Me-me gets everyone a drink.

Baby Enrico waves his hands when he sees me. "Carry you! Carry you!" he squeals.

I can't pick him up, so I kneel down next to him, and he gives me a sloppy kiss on the ear. Or maybe a bite. I'm not exactly sure, but he's still a doll.

"I like the black," Aunt Gina says, looking around.

"It's Mother's idea. Don't touch that side table—I think it's still wet," my mother says, rolling her eyes, and Aunt Gina laughs.

I go and stand by Pat.

"This is Pat," I announce to everyone.

Uncle Nunzio's the first one up, and he's shaking Pat's hand and hugging him and saying congratulations. Next comes Aunt Rosa, and then Uncle Ralphie and Aunt Fulvia. By the time Pat meets the whole family, he looks like he's been hugged to death.

The doorbell rings, and my mother gets up and opens it. Uncle Dominic is standing there, holding a box with a pretty red bow. He's wearing a new suit with a tie and shiny black shoes, not slippers.

He tips his hat. "Ellie," he says, "you look swell."

"Thank you," she says. "Won't you come in?"

I can tell how nervous he is, how nervous everyone is. It's like an air-raid drill: Everyone's waiting for the bomb to fall.

"Hi, Uncle Dominic," I say.

"Hi, Princess," he says.

"What's in the box?" I ask.

As if remembering, he looks down. "This is for your mother," he says, and hands it to her.

My mother undoes the ribbon and opens it, staring in silence.

"What is it?" I ask.

She displays the box. Two glistening lamb's eyes in tissue paper stare back.

For a moment everyone holds their breath.

Then my mother gives a wry smile and says, "Maybe you should hold on to them for a while. Help me keep an *eye* on Penny here."

Uncle Dominic grins at me, and everyone laughs.

I'll never know if it's because of the lucky bean in my pocket, but it's a night I'll always remember for what *doesn't* happen. Me-me doesn't ruin the chicken and Pop-pop doesn't tell bad jokes. Mother doesn't get mad and Uncle Dominic doesn't hide in his car and Nonny doesn't cry. For one night everyone acts normal and talks and eats and drinks and laughs. It's just plain old roast chicken with mashed potatoes and over-cooked peas and onions, but it's the best meal I've ever had in my whole life.

Everyone's got something to say. Me-me and Uncle Dominic talk about how they both love Florida, and Uncle Nunzio and Pat talk about business, and Aunt Gina and Mother talk about the best places to go dancing. Even Pop-pop manages to behave. He and Uncle Ralphie talk up a storm, and Uncle Ralphie promises to send him over a couple of good steaks.

After dinner, Uncle Nunzio pulls out a bottle of Italian *spumante*.

"For the happy couple," he says to my mother

and Pat. "May you have many years together."

My mother looks into Pat's eyes and leans in and kisses him.

Everyone claps, and Aunt Gina says, "You caught yourself a good one, Ellie."

Then Uncle Dominic stands up, and he looks tall and handsome, like the man I always knew he was.

"A toast," he says. "To our Princess."

"An angel if there ever was one," Uncle Ralphie adds.

"Heaven-sent," Pop-pop says.

"We don't care how many arms you got!" Frankie declares with a grin.

"To our beautiful Penny," my mother says, smiling at me.

Then *my whole family* stands up and shouts, "To Penny!" and clinks glasses. They sound like music, better than any song by Bing Crosby.

And me?

I just sit there and smile, my heart so full I think I'll burst, knowing what a lucky girl I am.

CHAPTER TWENTY-TWO

A Regular
Norman Rockwell Family

I still think of Heaven sometimes. These days my idea of Heaven is different, although it still involves butter pecan ice cream.

I want to say that my father's family came over all the time after that night, that we ate dinner and celebrated holidays together and everything. I want to say that we were like a picture postcard, a regular Norman Rockwell family, but that's not what happened. We just continued on as we always had, but it was all right somehow.

And Uncle Dominic? In my Heaven, Uncle Dominic's pulled himself together and is playing ball again. In my Heaven, he lives in a house and has a wife and a baby. In my Heaven, he's always smiling.

But real life isn't like my Heaven, so none of

that happened. He did move out of the car, though, and into Nonny's basement, which was kind of an improvement depending on how you look at it, although the car stayed in the yard.

Every once in a while I'll find him there, listening to the radio, watching the world pass by. And I always ask him the same thing.

"Remember that time we saw Dem Bums play at Ebbets Field?" I'll say.

"Sure," he'll say.

"Those were some good seats, right?"

He'll grin and say, "Best seats in the house."

And they were.

Author's Note

Although this book is a work of fiction, it was inspired by many stories from my Italian American family.

I was named after my great-grandmother Genevieve (Rosati) Scaccia. My great-grandfather Rafael Scaccia emigrated from Italy and entered the United States through Ellis Island. My uncles owned butcher shops and clothing factories and played bocce ball and their instruments after dinner. My great-grandmother had a "downstairs kitchen" in the basement of the house and sprayed Tabu perfume on the dogs and wore black. I had an eccentric cousin who lived in a car in the yard and carried "lucky beans." I remember many meals that took all afternoon to eat. Ricotta-ball soup and a dish we called *pastiera*, which was probably a variation of *pastiera rustica,* were family favorites.

The Penny naming story is a family legend. My maternal grandfather, Alfred Scaccia, tragically died when my grandmother was pregnant with my mother. Although my mother was named Beverly Ann, she was called Penny by her family. She was always told as a child that this was because her late father loved Bing Crosby and "Pennies from Heaven" was his favorite song. However, we learned the truth a few years ago. Apparently my grandfather knew he was dying and was heartbroken that he would never know his child. In his final days, he told everyone "That baby is just like a lost penny I'll never hold. A lost penny." But as in this book, my mother's story had a happy ending. My grandmother Mildred eventually got remarried to a wonderful man. Our very own Irish American grandfather, Mike Hearn is known for his sense of humor and love of ice cream.

The story of Penny's father is a hidden piece of American history. During World War II, President Franklin Roosevelt signed Proclamation 2527, which designated six hundred thousand non-naturalized Italians "enemy aliens." All "enemy aliens" of Italian descent were obliged to carry pink "enemy identification" booklets and turn in "contraband," including weapons, shortwave radios, cameras, and flashlights. In addition, they were warned against speaking Italian, "the enemy's language."

Poster issued by the U.S. government.

Although many of these Italian immigrants, like those of German and Japanese descent, were longtime residents and respected members of their communities and had American spouses and children, they were still under suspicion that they might conspire with the enemy. Many had their homes searched, over three thousand were arrested, and hundreds were sent to internment camps.

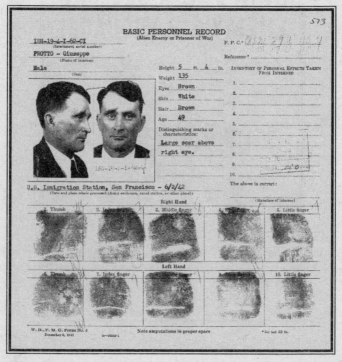

Records such as this one were kept on those in internment camps.

On the West Coast, all 52,000 Italian "enemy aliens" were put under a dusk-to-dawn curfew, and thousands were forced to move out of mainly coastal "prohibited zones." Famed baseball player Joe DiMaggio's father was not permitted to fish off the coast of California and was even forbidden to go to his own son's restaurant on Fisherman's Wharf in San Francisco.

Historian Lawrence DiStasi's book *Una Storia Segreta: The Secret History of the Italian American Evacuation and Internment During World War II* gives personal accounts of these painful experiences. It was not until 2000, after an exhibit called *Una Storia Segreta*, created by the Western Chapter of the American Italian Historical Association, drew national attention to this "secret story" and sparked intense lobbying by the Italian American community, that the U.S. government formally acknowledged these events when President Clinton signed Public Law 106-451, the Wartime Violation of Italian American Civil Liberties Act.

The story of the translator was inspired by a tale I heard years ago from a gentleman who claimed to have been Admiral Byrd's translator at the signing of the Japanese surrender at Tokyo Bay. He said he had interrogated Japanese POWs during World War II, and the information he learned had helped in choosing Nagasaki as a city on which to drop the atomic bomb. My uncle James

Hearn was stationed in Burma, now known as Myanmar, during World War II, and his experiences form the basis for Mr. Mulligan's story. Likewise, my great-grandfather Ernest Peck was a block captain during World War II, and my mother recalls having to put yellow-orange coloring in margarine during the war.

"Wringer arm" was an injury I first heard about from my father, a pediatrician. He said it was "the curse" of the pediatrician because it could be such a debilitating injury. Children could lose their arms as well as suffer extreme skin abrasions. I knew a woman who had lost her entire arm, up to the shoulder, when she was a child due to just such an injury.

Penny's mother's fears about polio mirrored the fears of many in the early 1950s, when the horror of polio was a reality. My mother was forbidden to go swimming in public pools for this very reason. Also, my mother had a terrible burn on her back from the tub, like Penny, and was treated with Scarlet Red.

Tales Calculated to Drive You MAD eventually became the infamous *MAD* magazine.

After their devastating loss in 1953, Dem Bums from Brooklyn went on to win the World Series in 1955. My grandfather saw several games at Ebbets

Field as a young man and remarked that it was one of the "smaller ballparks." In 1957, the Dodgers moved to Los Angeles, and soon after, Ebbets Field was torn down. But it still lives on in the hearts and memories of Bums fans everywhere.

A Family Album

My Italian great-grandmother Genevieve Scaccia (Grandma Jenny), in her signature black.

Penny's parents: my grandmother Mildred Hearn (Grandma) and grandfather Dr. Alfred Scaccia. This photo was taken on their honeymoon in Atlantic City, New Jersey, in 1938.

The postcard Grandma sent her parents from her honeymoon.

Grandma posing in her nursing uniform.

My mother, Beverly Ann Scaccia Holm (Penny), with her mother (far right) and her maternal grandparents—my great-grandmother Jennie Peck (Nana) and my great-grandfather Ernest Peck (Poppy).

Penny and her mother, my grandma.

Penny in one of the famous coats that her uncle Al DeGennaro had made for her at his factory.

Grandma with her second husband, Mike Hearn (Grampa), and my mother all dressed up for Easter.

Grampa Mike (at left) and his brother Jack playing college ball.

Penny with Poppy and Nana. This photo was taken on a vacation to Key West, Florida, where Nana was from.

Penny's cousin and best friend growing up, Henry Scaccia, Jr. (as an adult). He was an accomplished practical joker and once sent her a pair of lamb's eyes!

My mother, Penny, at about eleven.

RESOURCES

DiStasi, Lawrence, ed. *Una Storia Segreta: The Secret History of Italian American Evacuation and Internment During World War II.* Berkeley, Calif.: Heyday Books, 2001.

WEB SITES

The National Italian American Foundation: www.niaf.org.

World War II Internment: www.segreta.org.

Acknowledgments

The support I received from my family and the Italian American community in telling this story fills my heart so full that I think it'll burst. Trust me, I know what a lucky girl I am. *Mille grazie!*

First and foremost, I want to thank historian Lawrence DiStasi. His encouragement helped me give a small voice to the story of Italian Americans during World War II. Thanks to him and countless others, this part of American history is no longer a "secret story." Many thanks to Gina Miele at the Coccia Institute at Montclair State University; Fred Gardaphe at the State University of New York at Stony Brook; Julianna Barbato, Michael Marcinelli, Samuela Matani at the National Italian American Foundation; and the wonderful American Italian Historical Association.

A Brooklyn shout-out to everyone who helped me remember Ebbets and the Boys of Summer, including Claudette Burke at the Baseball Hall of Fame, Rick Whitney, John Lord, and Dem Bums fans at the Baseball Fever Web site.

My family has been enormously indulgent of my writing. Thanks to you all (especially for feeding me!): Frank and Mary DeGennaro, Dr. Ralph Scaccia, Donald and Rosalie Scaccia, and especially my cousin Sister Laura Longo. And a special thanks to my grampa Michael Hearn, who has put up with my endless phone calls.

I have been fortunate to have enthusiastic editorial support. My heartfelt thanks to Penny's godmother, the incredible Shana Corey, and Penny's other "aunts": Cathy Goldsmith and Kate Klimo and Mallory Loehr and Jill Grinberg.

Finally, I cannot begin to thank enough the one person who encouraged me to give this story life from its earliest days—my wonderful mother, Penny Scaccia Holm. As long as there are readers, your story will live on. The lucky bean is safe in my hands.

About the Author

JENNIFER L. HOLM is the author of two Newbery
Honor books, *Our Only May Amelia* and *Penny
from Heaven.* She is also the author of several
other highly praised books, including *Turtle in
Paradise* and the Babymouse series, which she
collaborates on with her brother Matthew Holm.
Jennifer lives in California with her husband
and two children. You can visit her website at
jenniferholm.com.